THE RHAPTA KEY

An Alex Hunt Adventure Thriller

URCELIA TEIXEIRA

Independently Published
by
Urcelia Teixeira

SPECIAL THANKS

To my husband Ricardo for the umpteen
mugs of coffee and shoulder rubs, and to
my three boys for being satisfied with
eating peanut butter sandwiches so
I could stay focused on
writing this book!

Receive a FREE copy of the prequel and see where it all started!

NOT AVAILABLE ANYWHERE ELSE!

Click on image or enter http://download.urcelia.com in your browser

PREFACE

Based on the true legend of Rhapta

About 2000 years ago, Rhapta was speculated to be the first real metropolis of Africa. The famed lost city was substantially known for its abundant produce of tortoise-shell and metal weapons amongst traders.

Rhapta soon became one of the wealthiest cities in the world and was mentioned in the Greco-Egyptian writer, Claudius Ptolemy's book "Geography."

The fact that he captured his findings in his writings proves that they knew of the city's existence as far back as 50AD.

But approximately 1600 years ago, at the peak of its existence, the entire city suspiciously disappeared.

The city vanished without any trace and with it took bounds of artifacts and architectural insights.

For years, archaeologists, scholars, and divers have been baffled by its disappearance.

The exact location is not known. However, it is believed to have been somewhere off the coast of Tanzania, near Mafia Island.

A recent accidental discovery by a diver in 2016 has the world excited with the prospect that he found Rhapta.

At present, they are in search of artifacts or any proof that the suspected ruins are conclusively ruled to have been the lost city of Rhapta.

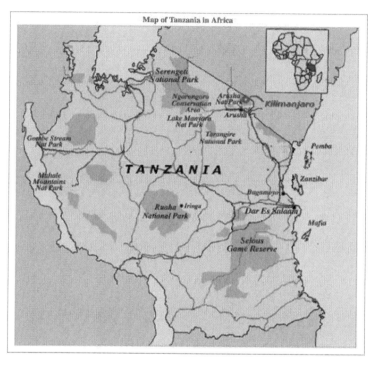

Map of Tanzania, Africa

CHAPTER ONE

ALEX

"**D**ad! I can't hear you! The line isn't very clear. Dad? What's going on? Hello? Dad are you there?"

The crackling noise on the other end of the phone stopped for a brief second. Alex listened as the single gunshot resounded over the phone line.

"Daddy? Dad! Please say something. Dad? Hello?"

Her legs went numb beneath her body. With her phone still in hand, she fell to the floor, unable to breathe.

She shut her eyes and mumbled a prayer out loud.

Her mind was a wicked flurry of questions. She had no idea what just happened. Convinced it was all in her head, she raised the phone to her ear again.

"Daddy?" Sounding like a five-year old, her voice trembling.

"Hello? Alex? Is that you?"

The voice startled her and ejected her off the floor. "Hello? Who's this?" She pressed the phone firmer to her ear.

"Alex, it's Eric. What did your father say to you?"

"What? Nothing, what do you mean? Where is he? I need to speak to him!"

"They took him, Alex! You need to find help! They shot me, and—"

"What? Who took him? Eric! WHO TOOK HIM? Hello? Are you there? Eric! Dad! Is anyone there?"

But Eric was silent and the all too familiar crackling sound at the other end of the phone echoed in her ears once again, blocking out any chance of hearing anyone speak. The sudden click and deafening silence confirmed the line had gone dead.

Her heart pulsed in her ears. The sequence of events that had just taken place was too hard to digest. With the phone still gripped in her hand she slumped to the floor, her legs folding numbly beneath her body. Paralyzed with fear not knowing what had just happened, tears rolled down her cheeks and dripped onto her phone's screen. Her shaking fingers scrolled through the menu on her phone as she searched for the last incoming number. Defeated she stared at the words: *number unlisted.* It was as if someone had punched her in the stomach. She banged the phone against her head forcing her brain to straighten itself out and in a moment of clarity realized whom she should call for help.

Her fingers fumbled with the phone as she dialed the only person she could think of. Several times the phone threatened to slip through her trembling hands that were now shaking uncontrollably. Just calm down Alex. Keep it together, she thought.

"Archaeology faculty, how may I direct your call?"

"Hello? Professor Keating please? It's an emergency."

"Who may I ask is calling?"

"Alexandra...Alex, Professor Hunt's daughter. Please, I need to speak to Professor Keating now! Please hurry. It's a matter of life and death."

Pacing the small room, Alex swallowed hard in an attempt to wet her parched throat. She waited anxiously as the call transferred.

"Alex? What's wrong?"

"Professor! I didn't know whom else to call. I don't know what to do. I...they, they took him, and Eric got shot and..."

"Whoa! Stop for a second. Calm down Alex. Take a breath. You're not making any sense. Who was taken, and who shot who?"

"My father, they took my father, and I can't make out if they shot him or, maybe they shot Eric, but I heard a gunshot and..."

"Okay slow down Alex. Where are you?"

"I'm at home. Dad called but I couldn't hear him clearly, and then Eric spoke saying they took him and then they shot him. You have to find him Professor!"

"Bugger. I knew your dad was up to something. Okay, make a cup of strong tea and sit tight. Let me make a couple of calls and see what I can find out, but for now try to keep it together. I'll get to the bottom of this as soon as I can."

"But Professor, I..." The line went dead in her ear.

"Hello. Professor," she repeated, but he had already put the phone down.

Irate, she threw the phone against the door. The back shot off and the battery slid underneath the couch. She swore under her breath at her own stupidity and knelt down next to the couch to retrieve it. Her fingers fumbled with the

4

battery and cell phone cover as she popped it back together.

"What have you gotten yourself into, Dad and where are you?" She said out loud clicking the cover in place.

Chewing her thumbnail she walked back and forth between the kitchen and the sitting room. Her clothes felt too tight all of a sudden, and she found it hard to breath. Her thumb left her mouth and fiddled with her now constricting medical bracelet on her wrist.

The thought of losing her father was too much for her to bear. Memories of her mother's death whirled through her mind. She frantically searched her desk for her pills and swallowed two, closing her eyes as she waited for the bitter sting to disappear and the medication to take effect. The prescription bottle in her hand stared back at her. These pills have become her lifeline.

Outside the rain gently tapped on the windowpane. She walked over and traced the soft raindrops down the cold glass.

How could this happen again? She thought. When her mum died, her entire world fell apart. It had been so long since she felt the rain on her face. If her father never returned she would have no choice but to go outside again. The thought of it left her cold. She couldn't face that. She wasn't ready.

She paced the room again, and fought against her taunting thoughts. She couldn't breathe. Not even with the exercises Dr. Jones gave her when situations like this called for it. Her chest felt tight, and her body appeared to be doing its own thing.

She reached for her phone and checked if she might have missed a call or message alert. She didn't. There were no missed calls and no messages. Disheartened she realized she'd go crazy waiting for the professor to get back to her. She hurried over to her father's large messy desk in the corner of the room. Her hands hastily thrust the piles of papers onto the floor.

She rummaged through the desk with vigor. He always left her a note or a clue when he went on a mission. It had to be there somewhere. She paused taking a couple of deep breaths as she continued the silent conversation in her head. He left three, maybe four days ago. He couldn't have gone far.

With trembling fingers she sifted through the loose papers on his desk but her search returned no note or anything else of significance. Nothing aside from a few student term papers, a couple of unopened letters, and a map.

Annoyed she paced the room back and forth between the door and the desk trying to convince herself that he was fine. She recalled their last conversation.

He had made a flippant comment about setting off to find the truth that will set them both free from the past.

But there was no truth to be found. The reasons would never be clear, at least not to her.

Feelings of him being in serious trouble gnawed at her insides. Something was wrong. She was certain of it.

A loud knock jolted her back to reality. She scrammed towards the front door almost tripping on the loose rug on the floor. She barely had the chain off and a drenched Professor Keating pushed past her into the house.

"Professor Keating, did you find him?" But instinctively she already knew the answer to her overzealous question. Why else would he be there in person?

"No, Alex I'm afraid I haven't, at least not yet. I did make some phone calls. My connections said he boarded a flight to Africa."

"Africa? What would he be doing halfway across the world! Are you sure?"

"I'm certain. We also found an email in your father's office from the University of Dar es Salaam requesting his help on a matter. They think they might have found the lost city of Rhapta."

"Tanzania? That's absurd, 'found Rhapta' what rubbish. Everyone is fully aware Rhapta is merely a myth. A fabled maritime city that disappeared off the face of the earth nearly 1600 years ago! It's nothing but a story some wannabe writer concocted to gain fame. This stupid city doesn't exist! Everything is a ridiculous myth, nothing more. No one has ever found any factual evidence of—"

"Apparently this time someone did find something. They claim to have found some pieces of ancient pottery and gold coins and some human fossils dating back two thousand years. The tests came back positive confirming the fossils are most likely from Rhapta. I think your father must have found something really significant and was kidnapped."

He paused briefly taking a deep breath before he continued.

"Alex, considering your mother lost her life chasing after precisely the same lost city, I realize this must be rather hard on you, but what if this is all true? What if all the facts and fables are true and Rhapta lies somewhere hidden or buried under the sea? Do you honestly think your parents would have spent their entire lives chasing after a phantom if they didn't believe any truth might lie within the legendary tale? Your father must have found something new that put him in this dangerous position. He's always had a nose for these things and he may finally be close to completing what your mother dreamed of doing all her life. She died trying, Alex."

"So he jumps on the first plane chasing this stupid fairytale only to land up dead like my mother. And what about me?

What am I supposed to do if both my parents end up dead?"

Alex felt her sweater tighten around her neck again as she struggled to breathe. She pulled at the neckband, but it proved futile and provided little relief.

"Alex, perhaps you need to sit down for a moment."

In an instance of insanity she tried ripping the sweater's neckband open. It was suffocating her and she fought to keep her emotions at bay.

"Alex, please. Sit down and try to stay calm. You will have to be strong now. We only have one way of finding your father."

She knew exactly what he was thinking and didn't like it one bit. Still tugging at her neck, she pre-empted his next sentence.

"You have to go to Tanzania and find him, Alex. You going is the only way."

She felt her body surge out of control. She was cold. No hot. Her heart beat fast and her lunch threatened to push up into her throat. The room spiraled out of control. Her stomach churned uncomfortably and a short moment later the room went black around her.

"**A**lex it's Dr. Jones. Can you hear me?"

Alex winced at her aching head as she tried opening her eyes. Dizzy and confused she groaned.

"Ah, welcome back. Try to relax for a bit. You fainted so just lie still for a moment. Here, have a sip of water."

The heavily sugared water left her tongue feeling furry.

"Better? You had a pretty hard knock on your head when you fell so don't try to stand up just yet."

"Alex, I'm truly sorry. I didn't mean to upset you. I —"

"Perhaps not the best time to apologize, Professor. I'd wait for her to find her bearings first. She'll be okay."

Alex rubbed the back of her head and propped her elbows underneath her body as she recollected the events that led to her fainting.

"Absolutely not! No, not going to happen. I CAN'T GO!" She ranted, catching the two men off guard.

"Okay calm down. You're confused." Dr. Jones responded.

"I am not going anywhere!" She repeated.

"Go where Alex?" The perplexed physician replied turning a questioning gaze at Professor Keating who had a suspiciously sheepish look on his face.

"Go where Professor? What's she talking about?"

"Africa, Tanzania to be more precise as a matter of fact."

"Africa? Have you lost your mind? To do what if I may ask?"

"To find her father. He's gone missing, and she's the only one who is equipped enough to find him."

"Oh no. No, no, no, no! No way on earth she can go gallivanting off to Africa! I'm afraid that is pretty nearly not going to be possible at all Professor Keating. Out of the question! Let me explain. She—"

"Yes, yes, Dr. I understand. She's still traumatized after having lost her mother much the same way and now the added upset of her missing father will be too much for her. I get it."

"No, as a matter of fact, I believe you do not. Unfortunately, this is a bit more complicated than a simple case of trauma. Alex has Agoraphobia. She can't leave the house. She's clinically Agoraphobic."

"Agora what?"

"Agoraphobia is an anxiety disorder characterized by an intense fear of certain places and situations, in normal circumstances set off by severe trauma. Alex hasn't been out of the house since her mother's death; apart from our exposure therapy sessions that is. Something like this would require an immense amount of courage and willpower for her to leave the house much less fly across the world in a cramped airplane."

Unimpressed by the textbook diagnoses, Professor Keating wasn't about to give up his fight.

"Alex, you may not have much of a choice in the matter. You would *have* to go. One of the archaeologists called me a short while ago. The people who captured your father are under the impression that he told you where the key is. If you don't go, they'll kill him. In short, they could black-mail you."

"That is absurd! It's ridiculous. Don't you understand? The key doesn't exist. Never did. There is no key!" Raising her voice more than she intended.

Alex shook her head. "I'm afraid you're going to have to send someone else or go yourself, Professor! I can't do it. It's not that I don't want to, I simply can't. You're going to have to help him, Professor."

"Alex, I wouldn't ask this of you if I wasn't convinced you're the best option we have right now. You know your mother's work inside and out. You've done all the research on Rhapta, and you speak the language fluently. That day, the day that your mother... you might have found Rhapta at that very moment and didn't even realize how close you were. Look, I understand this is going to be terrible for you but finding Rhapta was your mother's dream. The two of you were on the cusp of one of the world's most significant discoveries. We can't let her dream all go to waste. Don't allow her death to have been in vain. Your mother wouldn't have wanted you to pine away, locked up in this house forever. Archaeology is in your blood. It's your very DNA. You're a Hunt, Alex. It's your legacy."

Alex sat in silence as she felt the needle disappear into her arm. Whatever Dr. Jones injected made her feel like she was floating on air.

"Alex please, you have to. Do this for your mother."

Though now surprisingly calm Alex had every intention of punching Keating's lights out over his last sleazy salesman 'do this for your mother' stab. She could still recall the events of that day as if it just happened. She knew her mother would have wanted her to continue her life's work but to relive the entire ordeal on top of her father's disappearance was too much to ask. She paused her internal thoughts. There was a strong possibility that her father might still be alive. She couldn't sit back and do nothing.

As she pondered her fate the two men continued.

"Dr. can't you give her some miracle pill to take the edge off her situation; help her take control over this or something? If she doesn't go out there and find him it's very likely that her father will end up getting killed too. We have to put an end to this once and for all. These people are savages. They will never stop until they find the treasure and as long as they think her father or she has knowledge of the key or any of the so-called treasure they will keep going and might very well come after her here."

"Professor I mean no disrespect, but Alex and I have gone through years of therapy and behavioral treatments. She has her meds, but until she's psychologically ready, my hands are tied. Agoraphobia is not a physical ailment. It's a mental disease. One that either lingers forever or, best case, can be controlled with anti-depressants when the patient is ready. It is entirely a matter of being psychologically and emotionally ready. Once that happens, she can manage the disease as the symptoms occur. But, if you push a patient too hard at the wrong time, the consequences can easily go the other way and that could land her in an institution for the rest of her life. We simply have no way of telling where she's at right now."

The doctor paused and scratched his brow for a second before he continued.

"There was a recent case study so we might have a very slim chance here. Something we might be able to try IF she's willing. However, I must stress, this particular therapy method currently stands unproven, so I offer no guarantees. Theoretically, the treatment should work; if we're lucky."

"Sounds good to me, Dr. We should at least try. This is a matter of life and death so we might not have any other option."

"You two are talking as if I'm not here. May I remind you that it's my and my father's lives you're playing with here? You should send in the police, or the army or something, a team of professionals. I'm an archaeologist, not a soldier!"

"What's this therapy you mentioned, Dr.?" Keating ignored her and continued his conversation with the doctor.

"Well, the only other possible recourse is if you have someone accompany her. Preferably someone with a medical background who is stable and trustworthy that will help her through the panic attacks. It will have to be someone she knows she could trust and who will be with her every step of the way."

"Forget it." Alex suddenly surprised them. "I don't need a babysitter or a nurse. I'm quite capable of looking after myself. I'll go to Africa on my own, but only because my father's life depends on it. I'll fetch him and bring him back. Nothing more! No hunting down lost cities or relics or anything of the sort. I don't need to find Rhapta, and I am dead sure that I don't need the fame. Is that clear Professor?"

"Clear as daylight Alex. However, I just need you to think about the bit about not finding Rhapta and what you're walking away from. Just sleep on it. We have new evidence that the city does, in fact, exist. Lying somewhere in Tanzania waiting for us to unlock all her secrets and relics. The evidence is sufficient enough. As an archaeologist, you are duty bound to help us discover ancient history. A discovery of this stature can reveal valuable links to another history unknown to the world. Please consider the prospect. If not for me then do it at least for your parents."

Alex walked over to her father's antique desk and skimmed over the contents. History ran through her father's veins. She couldn't escape that. Keating was sure as heck pushing her beyond her comfort zone, but for the sake of her father, she really didn't have any other option.

Her mother, and obviously now her father too, believed this quest was worth risking their lives for. She should trust in their knowledge and experience and believe they might just be on to something big. Besides, Keating was correct of course. A discovery of this magnitude could provide valuable insights into new cultures and if this killed her too, then so be it.

Perhaps then all those treasure hunters who scour the world thinking they are on the verge of discovering ancient secrets and treasures will realize some secrets need to stay buried forever.

"Are you sure you can do this Alex?" Dr. Jones asked nervously. "You've made a lot of progress, but this might be too much for you to take on. Your meds will only do so much."

"Well, if the stuff has the same effect as what you just gave me, then, by all means, Dr., stock me up."

Professor Keating rushed to her side. "Alex, I'll send one of my best students with you as a backup and book you a first class seat. Anything to make the trip more comfortable for you. Just say the word."

"Students will weigh me down, Professor, I don't need them. I told you. I can do this on my own."

The doctor interjected. "Well, if I may Alex. I don't think that's wise. If you have an episode in the middle of a dangerous situation, the consequences could potentially be fatal. To have someone with you at all times will be vital to you getting through this."

Alex swept her hair out of her face and ignored his advice.

"I'll need something to knock me out on the plane and the ground team ready when I land, that's all. Oh, and a small supply of these meds you just gave me Doc. I'll manage the rest on my own."

"Alex, you need to be very sure this is what you want to do," the doctor cautioned again.

Her words echoed in her head. She had no idea how she was supposed to do this and why she agreed, but she knew she couldn't sit back and do nothing. As always, he was most likely right. She could never do this on her own and would probably end up dead, but she had to try.

"Thank you Doctor, but we are talking about my father's life. How can I not at least try? If his life depends on me risking mine to save his, then I have to do what anyone else in my position would have done. When my mother most needed me, I let her down. I am not about to do the same to my father."

Relic hunting was in her blood. She knew nothing else. Born to the famous Hunt explorers, escaping their legacy was impossible. She'd been to more countries hunting down treasures and ancient artifacts than most people will ever experience. Her childhood memories were not of birthday parties and learning how to ride a bicycle. Instead, her young life was filled with camel rides across the desert and swimming through crocodile-infested swamps.

Her father's words rang in her head. 'The excitement lies in the next chase. That's what makes life great.' No two days were ever the same. Most children only dream of going on wild adventures like she did instead of sitting through repetitious school lessons and bedtime routines. Just the world and all its experiences. A once in a lifetime organic education filled with firsthand lessons in eight different languages. Living with tribes in Peru or making clay pots in Egypt. Her life was never dull or without instruction.

The professor was right. Relic hunting was in her genes. She learned firsthand from the best explorers known to mankind. With the right ground team and resources, she could find her father and bring him home alive.

W hen Alex was eventually alone again, she sat down behind her desk. Her eye caught her emergency medical bracelet dangling around her wrist. Beneath the thin silver chain was the bright pink scar she got while sliding down the sharp sandy cliffs of the Kingdom of Mustang in Northern Nepal. Those mysterious caves were quite a find. That was, in reality, her first official expedition and she loved every living moment of the mission.

She caught herself smiling as she recalled the memories and realized how much she missed the adrenalin rush. The sheer exhilaration shooting through her veins when she conquered treacherous places where modern man had never been. The threat of danger contradicted by the mesmerizing tranquility that comes from being one with nature.

The silver medical tag around her wrist stared back at her. *Alexandra Hunt - Agoraphobic.*

For the last three years, she'd been staring at those words. Was this who she had become? Was this what the rest of her life looked like? She flipped the bracelet over and pushed it down against her skin. She was a Hunt. There's no escaping that, and if her mother were still alive, she'd tell her.

CHAPTER TWO

T he lukewarm tap water wasn't helping. Alex inhaled a series of shallow breaths and ran back into the bathroom cubicle. The dirty space was tiny. She stared at her reflection in the mirror and tried to calm her racing heart and mind by repeating the sequence of exercises Dr. Jones had given her.

Fifteen minutes later she climbed the aircraft's steps. In her head she recited the reasons for going on this trip, trying hard not to turn and run. Taking a few deep breaths in between each step didn't help much either. The plane was at capacity and evoked a sense of claustrophobia in her. She hated the confined space and people around her but much to her relief the airhostess showed her to a business class seat. Seated next to her was a man who looked ridiculously more nervous than she.

"First flight?" She asked him.

"Not quite but I guarantee you, without a doubt not exactly my place of comfort," he replied, still fumbling with his seatbelt as Alex opened the overhead above her seat.

"Oh, let me take that for you Miss Hunt," the friendly hostess stopped her.

"*Miss* Hunt? Oh... Uh, I beg your pardon. I was expecting —" The man in the seat stopped himself from blurting out the obvious.

"You were expecting what? A man?" Alex smirked as she watched him clumsily attempt to get up in the cramped space to greet her.

"Well, yes if I have to be truthful. Professor Keating told me to meet Alex Hunt, so I assumed... well, it's just that, Alex is a male name and, I..." scratching his head in a futile attempt to create a comeback.

"So they saddled me with a babysitter anyway. Great," Alex snapped back deciding to let him squirm for a bit. It wasn't the first time someone made the wrong assumption about her. Exploration wasn't for the faint-hearted and finding a female in her profession, was close to impossible. Her mother was one of the very few and they were always very careful about protecting Alex from the journalists who haunted them for the latest archaeological scoop. In hindsight, her parents' wisdom and foresight into the danger of exposing her identity in the tabloids were precisely what had kept her safe. In all probability it was the very catalyst to her mother's death.

"And who is the fortunate chosen one Professor Keating thinks is equipped enough to handle this expedition?" She asked the man sarcastically.

"Sam Quinn, at your service Miss Hunt," holding out his hand.

"And why exactly did Professor Keating think you'd be qualified to accompany me? Looking at you, I have the sense that planes aren't exactly your thing. How in heavens' name are you meant to climb down a shaft or slide through an underground tunnel if you're nervous about flying?"

"For one, I'm a huge fan of your parents, studied their every move and we all greatly respected your mother. Her death was a sad day in archaeology."

Alex ignored his comment. As far as she was concerned he didn't know the meaning of the word sad, but she was stuck with this guy and there was nothing she could do to change it.

"Well Sam Quinn, if you pull that strap any tighter you might sever your waist."

"You're right. I'm not the biggest fan of flying," tightening the seatbelt even more.

"I suppose you do this so often you might as well be driving a car. How many expeditions have you been on, Miss Hunt?"

"Unfortunately more than I care to count," she replied while fumbling with her safety buckle on her lap. The effect of the potent sedative was kicking in and slurred her speech. Perhaps she should have taken just one, she thought.

"Can I just say, Miss Hunt, I—"

"Alex, the name is Alex. Short for Alexandra, a female name." She cut Sam off, straight away regretting her irritation and bitter edge. Today, flying wasn't her thing either.

"Indeed yes Alex," clearing his throat. "As I was just going to say, I majored top of my class and am well equipped to have been selected to accompany you on this adventure. Your parents have been my inspiration and role models growing up. The very reason I fell in love with archaeology. I gave Professor Keating my word and well, how shall I put this? I'm aware of your condition."

That statement annoyed her even more, but she bit her tongue.

"Well, thank you Mr. Quinn, but judging from those clothes, this is, without doubt, your first rodeo. As for my condition, I can manage just fine, thank you."

He looked down at his crisp white collared shirt and black jeans and shuffled awkwardly in his seat.

"I figured if I'm going to die I should at least be dressed for the burial." Sam broke into laughter and Alex fought the urge to smile. At least the man had a sense of humor, even at his own expense.

"You, on the other hand, Alex Hunt, are dressed like GI Jane, ready to crawl through some tomb or chasm in the middle of a jungle. Do you always dress like this when you're flying?"

"Only when I try to blend in with the locals at my destination. Africa is unlike any other place you might have been to Mr. Quinn. The terrain is tough and the people, well, let's just say not all of them are friendlies."

Sam looked even more scared now.

"How do you mean 'not all of them are friendlies'? What does that mean specifically?"

"Don't worry Mr. Quinn. Dressed like that you might in effect scare them off."

Alex rubbed her eyes. Her eyelids appeared to weigh rather heavily as they started pulling south and she was certain her words were slurring a little too much. She pulled at the seatbelt in much the same way Sam did earlier and focused on her breathing again. It was the first time she set foot out of the house in over three years. If this wasn't facing her fears head-on, she didn't know what was. The corner of her mouth curled up ever so slightly. She loved Africa and could almost smell the familiar red dust that was such a big part of her childhood. To some extent she welcomed the exhilarated possibility of uncovering the truth about Rhapta and finding the key everyone believed existed. Discovering Rhapta was her mother's single greatest quest. She risked and lost her life for the sake of fulfilling her dream chasing after the legendary city.

Her father's face interrupted her thoughts. Losing her father was not an option. Her stomach turned at the thought and formed a lump in her throat. She swallowed hard and tried to control her trailing fears. *Look ahead, straight ahead. You can do this.* She recited in her head. She just needed to follow her father's last clues and bring him back home. That was it. Nothing more.

The pilot announced the emergency procedures and Alex's eyes followed the hostesses up and down the aisles as they did their last checks on the overheads before strapping into their seats.

She still wasn't sure how she had managed to leave her apartment that morning. If it weren't for Dr. Jones that drove her to the airport she in all likelihood would not have even made it to her front steps.

A nervous thought made her reach inside her khaki jacket and check that the round container of pills was still there. She started her breathing exercises and lay her head back against the headrest. Her hands gripped the armrests tightly as the plane took flight.

Moments later Sam Quinn's firm, muscular hand clasped hers. She wanted to pull away, but somehow the urgent need to rely on his strength pushed all her instincts aside. Alex glanced at him sitting stiffly in his seat with his eyes shut tight. Maybe he needed her courage too and in that very moment, Alexandra Hunt concluded that everything would be all right. Something in that moment told her that Sam Quinn would help her through the mission just fine.

She must have passed out shortly after takeoff as a passing passenger woke her by knocking her elbow with his kneecap. One by one the passengers scurried along the narrow aisle to disembark the plane. Still slightly woozy from the heavy sedation Alex unclipped her seatbelt and turned sideways to look at Sam where he patiently sat waiting in his seat. He seemed somewhat relieved that the plane was now safely on solid ground.

"Ah hello there. That was quite a nap, Miss Hunt. Here, I saved you some juice and a bread-roll."

The sedatives left her mouth dehydrated to the point where her tongue was stuck solidly to her palate.

"Thanks. Shall we head off then?" Alex replied while reaching for her backpack from the overhead.

"You're going to have to change out of those clothes Mr. Quinn. You won't last an hour in them. Please tell me you packed a carry on with some khakis."

"Right here. I've come prepared," rapping his rucksack now hanging on his chest like a baby carrier.

He looked like a naughty school child about to go to his first cub camp.

"Best you saddle up Mr. Quinn and let's shake a leg. You might have to change in the Jeep."

Alex couldn't resist rattling his cage a tad. This man was so obviously a novice at all of this. The horrified look on his face at the idea of having to change in a moving Jeep in the middle of rural Africa was just priceless. But it was a welcome distraction to her ever-troubled mind.

· · ·

The hot African sun hit her face the moment she stepped out of the plane onto the runway. Suddenly her feet were bricks of lead, glued solidly to the ground. Alex recalled her mother's face and the look in her eyes as they dragged her away. Her heart started racing, and her palms broke into a clammy sweat. She swallowed twice in a futile attempt to wash down the lump that found its way to her throat. Fear gripped her neck as doubt enveloped her mind. There was just no way she could go through with this. For a moment she contemplated turning around and heading back into the plane. She looked back but the crew had already raised the steps and swiftly closed the door behind them. Did they sense her trepidation? Perhaps they were told to do so.

Look straight ahead, Alex. You can do this, her inner voice whispered, but her legs weren't budging. No matter how hard she tried to walk, they just didn't react. She stood on the tarmac paralyzed for what seemed like hours.

Sam's firm supportive hand on her elbow gently nudged her forward.

"I've got you Alex. You can do this."

Suddenly the look in his eyes turned from Cub Scout to ranger, and Alex couldn't help but wonder if this hidden strength was precisely what Professor Keating had seen in him.

He nodded towards the bottle of juice that was still clenched in her hand, spurring her on to drink some more. She had never taken orders from any man except her father, but somehow her body decided to drop its defenses and follow his advice.

As if on cue her feet complied, and she felt herself walk steadily towards the passport control counter. A knee-jerk reaction had her greet the official in Swahili, which caught her entirely by surprise. She didn't expect to remember the language with such ease. She sensed Quinn was as surprised, or possibly impressed, but ignored it. The official's eyes paused firmly on her face, as he looked her up and down with suspicion. Why wouldn't he? She was a white English woman in the middle of Africa speaking fluent Swahili.

"Why are you in Tanzania?" He asked while flicking through her passport.

"I'm here on business," she replied in a calm voice.

"What business?"

"I work for a prestigious British University. I'm an archaeologist."

Her comment brought about a little bit too much attention from him, and he flicked back and forth through the pages of her passport as if he had lost something. He turned around and tilted his chin up at the supervisor behind him.

Without exchanging a single word, he pointed to something on one of the pages, yielding another incredulous look in Alex and Sam's direction. Alex guardedly glanced over to Sam whom stood two steps behind her and whom, without fail, also sensed that something was up. If those two officials were on the payroll of whoever kidnapped her father, they stood profoundly little chance of passing through the customs gates.

Alex felt her legs turn to jelly as the officials sized them up and down. Several minutes passed while the guard keyed in some letters on the somewhat antiquated computer. Africa surely was a third world country. Those things were archaic, she thought. The officer waited for something to pop onto the screen and turned to Alex. This time with a slight steely look in his eyes.

"How long are you staying?"

"Not long I hope. As soon as I manage to complete the study."

The stern look on his face told her that her answer wasn't quite what they were expecting from their interrogation efforts, so she added swiftly.

"I would guess about seven to ten days at the most."

Sam tugged at his collar and fiddled with his buttons.

"Don't!" Alex whispered to him over her shoulder.

"Don't show concern. You need to downplay the situation. These guys are looking for a reason not to allow us through."

The second official pulled out his mobile phone and disappeared behind the column behind his cubicle.

"Who is he calling?" Quinn whispered back nervously.

"My money is on the ringleader."

Alex paused. Her senses told her the official wasn't buying her story.

"Now listen closely, Quinn. Things are about to go bad for us. If we allow them to take us now, we're in trouble. How much cash do you have on you?"

"Cash? Oh, yes, okay cash," unzipping his rucksack's side pocket.

"Three-hundred quid."

"Great, I have three hundred too. Give me your passport. Hurry."

"Are you sure you're doing the right thing here Alex? Bribery is a serious crime, and we can land in a lot of trouble for this. If your plan backfires we—"

"I'm quite aware Quinn. I'm afraid this plan might be our only chance."

Alex slipped the wad of notes into their passports and slid the lot discreetly across the counter, looking the controller dead in the eye. Though her heart had quite positively sunk into the pit of her stomach, she dared not flinch.

The official reached across to take her bribe from her hand. Alex pushed down firmer on the passports deliberately not letting the payoff go just yet. His yellow tinted eyeballs met her firm stare. Words were not necessary in that moment. Alex could judge from his face that this tactic was not new to him. With his hands next to the payoff, the guard signaled for the head official to join him. It didn't take any convincing and, just as quickly as the mobile phone had appeared earlier, he slipped it back into his pocket.

Alex kept her eyes locked on theirs. Aware that Quinn still stood frozen behind her she sensed he might have stopped breathing altogether, but she dared not look away.

The head official cleared his throat and handed the ink stamp to the guard who quickly tucked the notes under some papers. Alex watched nervously as he stamped both their passports. He slid them across the counter before slipping the cash out from beneath the papers and into his pocket.

"Next!" He shouted signaling for them to walk through the gates.

This time it was Quinn who couldn't move.

"Come. Let's go!" Alex elbowed him.

Her legs resembled the jelly in Mrs. Parsons' Christmas trifle but somehow the adrenaline of her newfound corruption talent propelled them forward with the agility of a gazelle.

"Keep up Quinn. We're not out of the woods just yet. We need to find our way to the pickup. Hurry!"

"What about our luggage?"

"We'll have to send someone for it later. We need to go now Quinn."

Soundly aware of several police officials' watchful glances, Alex walked on. She suspected that they might have already been informed to either keep an eye on them or wait for another opportunity to gain their own payoffs.

"I can't believe you pulled that off. That was amazing! How did you know they were going to take the bribe? Where did you even learn how to do that?"

Quinn's admiration did not quite grab Alex's full attention. Her senses were on high alert while she tried to maneuver them through the busy airport.

"Where are we going?"

"The pickup point. We have to find our way out of here. Let's just hope the ground team got the message and has someone ready and waiting. My father always had a knack for rounding up the best ground teams. But I don't have the foggiest if Professor Keating managed to relay a message to them or not. Unfortunately, we do face the odd chance that they were also captured or worst, killed when they kidnapped my father."

"And what happens if the ground crew isn't at the pickup?"

"They had better be waiting for us, or we are as good as dead. Africa is spectacularly beautiful but if you face its bad side the people can be your worst enemy. And judging from our first encounter, we're not likely to be off on a good footing. Someone will be waiting for us, I'm sure."

Quinn's tanned face drained a pale grey as he realized, what he thought was going to be a walk in the park, might in fact change his life forever.

Once through the airport's south end, the pair sneaked through the maintenance exit. This was the one spot in the entire airport not covered by a surveillance camera—knowledge Professor Keating somehow acquired. Alex dared not ask how. Judging from how quickly those officials took their bribe it was evident Africa had a different set of rules. She guessed he bought the Intel in much the same way she had just bought their entry into the country. Chuffed it appeared they lost the entourage, they stopped briefly to check they were still undetected.

Alex shot up a silent prayer that someone would be waiting for them at their pickup point. The end of the corridor dragged closer as they hurriedly moved towards the heavy steel door at the end of the passage and flung it open.

"Lakicia!"

The sound of her Swahili name overwhelmed Alex with immense relief. It had been so long since she'd heard anyone call her by her tribal name and she instantly recognized the voice.

"Jelani! You are a feast for my eyes, my old friend."

"Me too Lakicia. You have been gone for too long but come, we go now. We talk later. Militia they follow me. Ol' Jelani still faster," chuckling without a care in the world.

"I've missed you, my friend," she continued in his native tongue.

"Lakicia, you still remember? How many years and you still remember the language?" Jelani replied in surprise as he smiled to reveal a mouth missing a number of teeth.

"The two of you do realize that I don't speak a word of Swahili, so I frankly don't have a clue what you're saying. But be that as it may, I'm hoping you remember we have some assailants chasing us!"

Alex was so caught up in seeing her childhood friend again that she totally forgot about Quinn and the imminent danger behind them.

"Sorry Quinn. Meet my old friend, Jelani. We spent a lot of time together as children. His father was my father's trusted *mshauri*. He taught him everything he needed to learn to survive here in Tanzania. Jelani, this is Sam

Quinn. Apparently he's one of the top students at the University, or so I'm told. I'm trusting he has a hidden skillset to help me find my father underneath all this."

"I am not so sure about that, Lakicia. His clothes say the opposite," Jelani joked, letting out another chuckle as he sped off down the dirt road.

"Okay, okay. I still can't understand what the two of you are saying, but I am no one's fool. I'll change my clothes," Sam joked back.

CHAPTER THREE

CHARLES

"We know who you are Professor so give us da key! We can do dis da easy way or da hard way."

Charles Hunt's jaw throbbed under another punch in response to his silence. He was convinced the last blow dislodged his tooth. The harsh metal taste of his blood filled his mouth as he tried catching his breath. Charles spat a ball of bloody saliva in his attacker's face.

"So... den you choose da hard way? You stupid scumbag!"

The blow to Charles' stomach doubled him over, and he struggled to breathe again. The man circled around Charles and went in for another punch. His legs gave out beneath his tortured body. The giant behind him tightened his grip on his bound arms forcing his body upright as another blow thrust into his stomach. That one hurt.

"We can do dis all day, Professor. Your sissy assistant not here to rescue your sorry ass. Better give up and tell us where to find da key."

In spite of his broken English, the attacker's voice was hoarse with impatience. Charles wasn't sure how long he could keep up the torture. He wasn't the spring chicken he was thirty years ago. Back then he would have given this buffoon a whipping he would never forget.

The blood gushed from his swollen eyebrow, which made it nearly impossible to see. He recalled how the rebels ambushed them in the village and how all chaos had broken loose after that. Searching his memory, he remembered how the ground team scattered as they sought hiding and how he had lost sight of Eric when they pulled the black hood over his face. There was the gunshot; one single bullet he couldn't quite make out where it came from or whom it was intended to hit. Was it possible that it was Eric who got shot? If not then there was a distinct possibility they were busy torturing him for information too. And if they were he was pretty sure Eric would die regardless. The poor fellow didn't have a clue where Rhapta was. Charles had always been very careful not to share too much information with him.

In hindsight perhaps this was now Eric's saving grace or maybe the very thing that would get him killed. Unless he was already dead. Izzy might have been right all along. The boy was not hardened enough to cut it in their line of work.

Either way, Charles was as good as dead too if they had captured or killed the lad. There wasn't a doubt in his mind that he did his job of relaying communications to the uni well, despite the fact that he disappeared into town on more than one occasion. What Charles wasn't convinced on was whether Eric managed to get a distress call out to Keating. Charles instantly regretted not sharing his location sooner. He wasn't even sure if Alexandra had heard anything when he tried calling her. It wasn't looking good for him. He'd have to think of something to at least buy him some time even if it only provided a breather from the punches.

His attacker stopped to wipe the sweat off his face and guzzled down a jug of banana beer. It afforded Charles the slightest gap to catch his breath before the man went over and spat a mouthful of beer in his face.

"So you quiet Professor? You say nothing?"

"I don't have the key. I'm here on personal business. I told you. I've come looking for my wife."

"Ha! Your wife!" Spitting out another mouthful of the drink as he chuckled in ridicule.

"Everyone knows your wife is dead Pro-fes-sor! She did not want to give up da key either you idiot."

Charles ignored his parody. He only had one shot at this. If what he was planning worked he'd have to save his energy for what lay ahead. It was a long shot but worth a try, so he waited patiently for the mockery to end before he spoke again.

"No, she's not. My wife isn't dead."

"What you say, white man? You think I'm stupid?"

"No, I don't. My wife is alive. She's not dead. She called me from here a week ago, but the line was too bad and went dead. So I've come here to look for her. If I find her, I find the key. Then you can take the damn thing and let us go."

Charles dared not look up at his kidnapper now. He was certain he would spot the deceit in his eyes, so he kept looking down at a stone on the ground between his feet. The same stone that kept his focus away from the brutal force of the punches. It helped him focus on Alexandra, reminded him of the time they had escaped to the beach after Izzy died. They had spent the morning picking up pebbles on the beach and placed it on Izzy's grave. She loved the ocean.

"Aikôna, that is a lie!" Charles heard the accusations from behind him. "Sir who says he's speaking the truth? He's a liar."

The giant who held Charles up had spoken for the first time. Charles listened as the two men argued. They spoke

Swahili. Charles wasn't fluent but he deduced they were accusing him of lying. All he could think of was escaping and getting back to Alexandra. His mind traveled back to when she was a little girl playing with the village kids. She picked the language up so quickly.

But his troubled thoughts were interrupted as the giant jerked his head back and forced him to make eye contact with the rebel leader.

"If I find out you lie about dis Professor, I slice your throat with my knife."

As if that wasn't clear enough he emphasized his threat by spitting in Charles' face before he walked off.

Grateful that his bluff paid off Charles silently sighed with relief. His exhausted body ached from the beating. His feet dragged trails in the sand behind him as the giant pulled him back towards his makeshift bamboo cell.

The sharp stones purposefully laid down to extend his torture, pierced his body as the rebel threw him onto the ground. Charles slumped down sideways onto the sharp stones and tried to shuffle onto his feet by leaning back against the bamboo rods. As if the rebel needed to prove once more who was in charge he kicked Charles from behind causing him to fall face down onto the stones.

"Blooming jerk!" Charles shouted as he spat out another mouthful of blood.

His attacker's foot pushed down heavily on his back forcing him to lie flat onto the jagged rocks. The slicing sound of his knife taken out of its sheath triggered Charles' body into a curled up ball as he waited for the imminent stabbing.

He might have underestimated the giant. Perhaps his bluff failed and this marked his end. Charles shot up a silent prayer as his life flashed before his bleeding eyes. But in that moment a vigorous tug at the rope around his bound hands left it snapping into pieces instead. The ropes ripped and scattered on the ground beside him, freeing both his hands. Instinctively his hands covered his head as he curled back into a fetal ball, convinced the giant had missed his mark. He readied his body for the fatal stabbing, but nothing happened.

For the first time, Charles raised his head and faced the giant who towered above him. He guessed him to be roughly six feet, at least, with every bit the physique of a professional football athlete. His khaki military shirt and trousers carried stains of fresh blood mixed in with months of dirt. His teeth were brilliant white against his black, sweaty skin.

Charles looked full into his perpetrator's yellow-tinged eyes and watch as he turned to fiddle with the lock of the bamboo door behind him.

"Water. I need water if I'm to have energy to find my wife."

The giant paused and Charles felt his heart skip multiple beats. They wouldn't let him die. Not with him being the only way they'd find the treasure. Surely he had them cornered. Minutes later the giant arrived with a bucket of water and a lump of *ugali*. Charles relished inwardly. He still had it. Age might not be on his side but guts he had until the day he died, and this wasn't that day.

The murky water stared back at him. It looked disgusting but he had been without food and water since his capture. If he were to get an opportunity to escape he'd have to eat and drink whatever they gave him. The giant rolled the lump of doughy bread between his dirty, sweaty hands and tossed it at Charles.

"You gonna look or eat white man?"

Charles had caught the ball of Tanzanian staple. The bread looked and smelled revolting. The dough was warm and nauseatingly gooey and quite possibly days old. He took a bite nonetheless, unable to deny the hunger pangs that suddenly ambushed him. The maize and milk mixture should at least sustain him for a little while.

The rebel cursed under his breath and dropped the bucket of water hard on the ground causing the pail to almost topple over. Half the brown, muddy water spilled over the sides.

With newfound bravery Charles mockingly saluted him. Unimpressed, the rebel reciprocated by forcibly ejecting his saliva in Charles' face.

Charles fought the urge to sling a long string of unsavory words back at him, but he held back. He needed to keep his wits about him now. He was ahead in the game, and these guys were fully aware but the giant's eyes told him he'd far rather kill him than find treasure. Charles was kept alive only because he was ordered to do so.

He reminded himself of his mission. He needed to eat and rest to build up his strength enough to endure his escape. He had one chance tomorrow when they all went off looking for Izzy, her phantom at least.

Resolved to escape Charles chose not to react and taunted the rebel by taking a bite of the dough. He will show no fear. It worked and Charles was left alone.

<hr />

Although the sun already sat quite low, its rays beat down on the bald patch on the back of Charles' head. If he'd hazard a guess he'd peg the time to be somewhere in the late afternoon. The African sun was generally at its hottest around then. But there was no way of knowing for certain since they stole his wristwatch along with the rest of his belongings when they captured him.

That watch was his last chance of being found. With any luck, they weren't smart enough to figure out that it had a built-in GPS tracker. If they haven't switched the tracker off yet, the signal should lead the ground crew straight to him. As long as he was with the rebels, that is, and as long as the ground crew was still alive.

Charles scooped another few sips of water in his filthy hands. Most of the sand and grit now lay at the bottom of the bucket. The water still tasted and smelled like stinky feet, but it was water nevertheless and welcoming under the sweltering heat.

Night would fall soon, and the temperature will drop and most likely bring a lot of rain. If they left him in his cell, he'd be in for a long wet night. Before long the heat and exhaustion got the better of him, and he passed out. A loud bang brought him back to a conscious state and moments later the sound echoed through the air again. Not quite sure what woke him, Charles sat up and looked around. He noticed the sun was just about to set. Clusters of rebels scattered in all directions running for any form of cover behind their bunkers and the trees. The sound of cocking guns and shouting commands came from everywhere.

It dawned on Charles that they were under attack, most likely a rival group.

Charles lay down flat on the ground. The sharp edges of the rocks pierced his abdomen. He was completely exposed. The giant was nowhere in sight. He was an open target in that cell. One stray bullet was all it took. He thought of lying still and faking his death. More shots fired off in his direction. They were closing in on him.

He looked around. The coastal regions were relatively familiar to him after all the years of exploring, but without being privy to his exact location there was no telling where he was. If he could get the lock open he could choose any direction and just run. He could seize this raid to aid his escape.

Faking and waiting wasn't an option. He had to break out of there. He picked up a sharp rock and smashed it at the lock. It didn't budge so he kicked hard into the bamboo poles. The sharp rocks sliced through his other foot sending pangs of pain up his leg. He was too weak to kick through the strong bamboo poles. Another bullet flew over his head as blood gushed from his injured foot. He'd bleed to death if he didn't stop it so he ripped his shirt in two and bound both his feet. With some relief beneath his feet, he hit a rock against the lock again but stopped when he spotted some of the rebels taking cover behind him. In high alert they sat silently waiting on their pending attackers.

"Hey! Get me out of here!" Charles shouted only to be ignored as more bullets flew past his head.

Keeping an eye on the rebels Charles spotted the giant squatting against the large tree directly behind him.

"Hey! Get me out of here!" He shouted at the giant.

"Get down!" The giant shouted back.

Charles did so just as a series of bullets left the giant's gun and whisked past his head to three insurgents that had crept up behind Charles. The giant confirmed where his loyalty lay by killing two of them in an effort to keep Charles alive. He was after all their ticket to a sizable fortune when they found the key.

"Tell me about da key old man! You die today. Where is da key?"

Charles cursed the key. He should have guessed the guy was looking after his own interests. Every archaeologist and relic hunter known to man scoured the coast in the hope of finding the infamous lost city of Rhapta and all its treasures.

"Nothing but a fairytale you idiot!" Charles responded.

"I not believe you! Where's the key, old man? You say NOW!" He pointed his gun at Charles.

"Believe me. I am telling you the truth. We have no proof of a key ever existing!"

"You a liar! There is lots of gold. You have the key. Where is it?" The giant continued relentlessly as another series of bullets left his gun.

"Get me out and I'll show you!"

"You lie I kill you! This no joke!" The giant warned as he moved towards unlocking the cage but quickly ducked behind the tree again to escape another fierce rain of crossfire.

Charles fell to the ground. He was in their direct line of fire.

"I can't show you if I'm dead! Get me out of here you idiot!"

The giant knew he was useless dead. Firing several defense shots he sneaked up and stuck his key in the cell door's lock to free Charles.

"On your feet, white man!" He shouted; challenged to open the lock under pressure.

"Have you gone altogether bonkers? You're going to get us both killed! Give me the keys!"

"Shut up white man! You know nothing. Get up!" Jerking both the cell door open and pulling Charles to his feet with one foul motion.

Before Charles even had the chance to object the giant pulled him behind the tree. The rough act over the sharp stones ripped the makeshift shirt bandages off and sliced fresh cuts into his feet.

"I need shoes. I can't run like this."

"Ah, *udhi,*" the giant spat at Charles to sod off and looked down at the blood gushing from the soles of Charles' feet. A dead victim lay on the ground behind a nearby tree. Within seconds he had pulled the corpse closer by his shoulders and removed his shoes.

"Here," slamming the shoes against Charles' chest before killing another enemy over his shoulder.

"Hurry white man. Put on dem damn shoes."

He fired off another series of bullets from his AK47 rifle and Charles ducked quickly, dead man's shoes in hand. The thought of putting on a mutilated corpse's shoes chilled him to the bone and he stared at the dead guy with guilt.

"White man! I say, put dem on! He no need dem anymore. We go!" Firing another round before reloading his gun.

Of course he was right. The poor sod was dead, and his feet were bleeding. Charles tightened the bandages and reached over to remove the stiff's socks. The shoes were too big, but it was better than nothing.

Charles jumped up and took cover behind the rebel's gigantic physique. But seconds later his enormous weight pinned him flat on the ground.

"Hey, Giant shove off!" But he didn't move and neither could Charles. He felt a thick hot liquid trickle onto his face and down the side of his cheek. It was blood. The giant got himself shot in the head and had fallen back onto Charles.

Flat out disgusted by a dead man lying on top of him, Charles tried frantically to move out from underneath him. He failed at pushing him off and tried again, but the giant weighed more than a pregnant elephant.

Footsteps approached and Charles stopped. If he lay still under the giant, they might not spot him, so he tucked his head, arms, and body under the giant and waited.

Relieved, his tactic worked and the enemy walked away. This was his chance. He had to move the giant off of him before the rebels came looking for him. In his mind, getting him off was a simple case of physics. If he pushed only from one end instead of from the center, he should roll off. In theory at least, but it might just work. It was his only option.

After three solid attempts and with all his remaining strength drained, Charles managed to lift the giant off his body. The welcome sensation of his lungs filling up with air had him gasping and back on his feet under the nearby tree from where he surveyed his surroundings with caution.

Most of the rivals had already left, and one by one the rebels were slowly coming out from their hiding spots.

Thankfully they hadn't as much as looked his way. Charles turned and bolted between the trees as fast as his sixty-something injured body could take him.

With night upon him, the dark woods were a welcome advantage as he disappeared out of sight into the night.

CHAPTER FOUR

ALEX

"Aah no worry Pommie. We lost dem far behind. Ol' Jelani da best at shaking danger."

They sped off from the airport, and Alex glanced at Sam where he sat in the rear of the open Jeep. He was still looking back through the trail of dust and not entirely convinced by Jelani's overconfident assurance. Sam nervously wrapped his now white knuckles around the bull bar of the vehicle in a pointless attempt to stick to the seat and not be flung out around the next corner.

Alex suppressed a giggle as Jelani purposefully flattened his foot on the pedal, all the while watching for another reaction from Sam. Sam's once starched white shirt was left tainted with a red-brown film of African dust kicked up by the back wheels next to him. Alex knew that when

Jelani drove a vehicle, one had to hold on for dear life to stay seated. To attempt anything other than holding on was lunacy, much less change into different clothing. The poor sod was in over his head and had no idea how to survive in Africa. He was probably too focused on his dream to meet the famous Professor Hunt, Alex thought.

She closed her eyes for a second, sending up another prayer that her father was okay and still alive.

"He'll be okay Lakicia. Your old man is a warrior remember? He has always found a way to get out of a sticky situation. We'll find him. I promise."

Jelani still had a knack of knowing the very thing that went on in her head.

"Your intuition has always been as sharp as a knife, my old friend. I suspect precisely the reason why Dad always trusts you to lead the ground team on all his expeditions. Your father's skillful training stands you in good stead."

"I learned from the best Lakicia but I promise you, your father is alive and well."

"I hope you're right Jelani. If he does manage to free himself somehow, he will try to find the village. I guess the question to ask should be whether he would be able to determine how to find it without knowing his exact location."

Jelani fell quiet for a while. His always-smiling face suddenly turned pensive. Being her childhood friend, he primarily grew up with her parents in the village. Izzy was so determined in finding that stupid key that Tanzania, initially meant to be just another quick expedition, turned out to be more like their long-term home. Jelani's mother had died of malaria when he was just a toddler so naturally they had stepped up to the plate and took him in.

"I'm sorry I couldn't protect her Lakicia. She was like my very own mother to me. I would have saved her if I could. I did try to track her but ... well, you know what happened. And now I've gone and done the same to your father."

"Oh, Jelani don't!" Touching his arm.

"None of this was your fault," she added.

She felt her chest suddenly tighten as the horrific memories of the past and now, her father's kidnapping flashed through her mind. Jelani's perplexed look didn't help and what he said next, troubled her even more.

"Everything happened so quickly. I'm still not sure I quite understand how your father's kidnappers even found out where we were."

"What do you mean 'you don't understand how they found you'?"

"Just like I said Lakicia. You know we're always careful with being followed and covering our tracks to the village.

We had a big cattle theft some time back. So my father thought we should rather move the village to a new spot a little bit further down the river. No one knew of our new location. We have watchers in the trees all day and night."

"Yet they attacked?"

"Exactly. We've mastered protecting our villages and have been doing this for decades. Tracing us is nearly impossible.

"I see your point, Jelani. What about access via the river? Could they have come in from the other side perhaps?"

"Not a chance! That's impossible. This river spot is perilous. At the moment the crocs' breeding ground is in the area so swimming will be a suicide mission. They would have had to use boats, but then we would have seen them. I guess we'll never discover the truth. No point now in any case. We can't change what happened. We lost four of our warriors, and your father is still missing."

Alex tugged at her seatbelt. Feeling the wind through her hair barely satisfied the urgent desire to breathe more air into her lungs. A massive wave of panic sneaked up on her. They took her father and the thought of him lying dead somewhere was devastating. But this affected Jelani too.

"And your father, Jelani? Did he... is he alive?"

"Ah yes of course," he giggled with a proud smile.

"The Chief is as tough as coconuts. He would never lose a fight. He showed them rebels all right. But unfortunately the fight was long since over and not his to have. They only took your father and left. Almost as if they came just for him and nothing else."

"And Eric? Where was he when all this happened? He took over the phone when Dad tried calling me, and he said they shot him, but then the phone went dead. Is he dead?"

"Shot?" A very surprised Jelani exclaimed.

"Not to my knowledge. Saw him running off with my own two eyes, Lakicia. And the other day in the city, I could have sworn he was buying rum at the liquor store. I've been looking everywhere for him since."

"Well, we're going to have to find him before they do. He might very well have some idea where they are holding Dad captive. I just hope we locate him before...well before they—"

Alex couldn't bring herself to even speak the words or think the unthinkable. Losing her Dad the same way she had lost her mother was not an option.

A sudden surge of overwhelming anxiety and fear engulfed her. The choking sensation in her throat had her tugging on her shirt collar. Her hands were sweaty and trembled uncontrollably, and her heart pounded in her chest. She reached for her pills inside her jacket, but her pocket was empty. She dug deeper. Still nothing. She crossed over to the other pocket thinking she might have confused the two but this one turned up empty as well. She patted down her pants pockets, and unclipped her seatbelt in an attempt to lift her body off the seat, hoping that the bottle had slipped out onto the seat beneath her.

"Alex, have you lost your mind? Sit down!"

Alex was vaguely aware of Quinn shouting at her from the backseat.

"Where did you learn to drive, Jelani? For the love of Pete slow down!" Sam yelled out when Jelani hit a pothole and Alex was almost thrown out.

Jelani didn't seem to know the brakes even existed and merely raised his foot off the accelerator.

"Stop, you damn lunatic. Alex will fall out! Hit the brakes!"

Sam's words were only just spoken when Jelani slammed on the brakes causing the Jeep's rear to slide out sideways and veer off the sandy road. A couple of branches hit Alex across the face as she fell back into the seat. Jelani frantically attempted to adjust the steering wheel into the opposite direction in an effort to gain control of the now out of control car. The vehicle lunged to the other side and lost its grip on the soft sand and then rammed through the bushes before it hit a large thorn tree.

Alex became aware of her body ejecting from her seat before it became buoyant through the air and then thumped down hard onto the ground.

Her head spun and an intense pain ensued from somewhere she couldn't quite make out. Exhaling a deep groan, she managed to sit up. Fresh, warm blood ran down her temple and more trickled down the center of her nose. Her wrist hurt when she pushed herself up from the ground. She struggled keeping her balance and fell back down against the tree.

"Jelani, Quinn, Jelani!" She called out in a voice that didn't sound like hers. Her eyesight was strained by the blood blurring her vision, so she tried wiping some away with the back of her hand. That didn't help. Instead, she now couldn't open her eyes at all. She pulled her shirt from around her waist and wiped away the blood.

A very faint moan and a rustle in the nearby shrubs had her squint for better visibility.

"Jelani? Is that you?" She asked still wiping the gushing blood from her eyes.

"Alex... it's me. Are you okay?" Quinn's strained voice came from behind the shrubs.

"Quinn! Yes, no. I'm not sure."

"Hang on, I'm coming."

She watched as he stumbled to his feet pulling off bits of shrubbery as he made his way to her.

Sam cursed out loud and then added, "you're bleeding buckets, Alex! Stay down."

Seconds later Quinn ripped his sleeves off his fancy shirt and turned them inside out before wrapping it tightly around her head.

"Sit back. We have to stop the bleeding. Try not to move."

"Jelani... where is Jelani?"

They both paused for an instant, straining their ears in the hope of hearing Jelani move somewhere, but there was nothing but a deadly silence.

"Stay here. I'll go look."

Sam, naturally still dizzy from the crash, walked across to the upside-down Jeep that lay under a nearby tree.

Alex willed her thoughts into Jelani still being alive. Without him and the sheltering safety of his village, they'd be vulnerable to the rebels and all sorts of prey. It wouldn't be long at all before they'd be captured—or dead.

The screeching noise of steel against steel followed by a muffled bang had her look up towards the wreckage. Her sight was completely blurred. Dependent only on her hearing she turned her head and detected another muted unidentifiable sound coming from somewhere behind her.

Still leaning against the tree trunk, she wiped her eyes once more before turning her head towards the direction the huffing sounds came from. With slightly less blurred vision from behind the thick tree trunk she spotted movement in the shrubbery about fifty to a hundred meters behind her.

"Quinn!" She whisper-shouted towards the wreckage just as another chuffing noise came from the bushes behind her.

Alex recognized the sound to be a cat of some sort, lions or perhaps cheetah.

She looked back at the wreckage. Sam was still nowhere in sight. Her mind raced with options. They were in the middle of the African Savannah with just about every wild animal roaming about. Most tourists would pay top dollar to spot any one of the animals, and yet here they were, about to become their dinner!

She had a vague idea of their location being somewhere close to the village that was on the banks of the river. With the sun just about set it meant that they would be on the immediate path to the river and that meant only one thing; they were near a watering hole. Most of the animals would have returned from the river by sunset to find shelter for the night or, in the case of a lion, readying itself for a hunt.

Either way they were in danger. Alex wiped her eyes again hoping to lay eyes on Sam who was still not back. She dared not call out to him again. Whichever cats were hiding in those bushes would be alerted by any loud noise. While her eyes were fixed dead on the spot behind her, another slight movement came at her from the Jeep's direction. It was Sam walking towards her from the wreckage. As he met up with her, Alex noticed Jelani's limp body in his arms and moments later, Sam lay Jelani on the ground next to her. He was oblivious to the fact that they were prime prey to lurking carnivores.

Alex swallowed twice trying to force the hard lump in her throat down as her eyes teared up at the sight of Jelani's limp frame.

"He was pinned under the Jeep, Alex. He's still breathing, but he might very well have internal injuries."

While Alex made every attempt to speak she couldn't. Her lips were moving, but there was no sound coming from her throat. She tried again but managed to only utter the tiniest of squeaks. She had to somehow stop Sam from talking and warn him about the lions. With a shaking hand she lifted her finger in front of his mouth signaling for him to be quiet, but it was too late. The lions made their presence known with a loud growl.

"WHAT— WAS — THAT?" Sam mouthed as more growls filled the air.

Still unable to get any sound from her voice Alex quietly cleared her throat in the hope that this time she'd be able to speak.

"Lions," she croaked as she successfully managed a soft, hardly audible whisper.

"Have some water. I kind of need you to speak right now Alex," Sam whispered back forcing some water down her throat.

"Tell me I didn't just hear you say it's a lion."

Alex gulped down the water and nodded. "I'm not sure, but yes, I suspect so. They're not a threat right now. Just keep your voice down. The wind is in our favor but we can't stay here, Quinn. We're going to have to find shelter and quick."

"What do you mean a LION?" He said with a tiny note of angst in his voice.

"We are in the middle of the African bush, Quinn. Lions and cheetah and all sorts of other wild animals are all around us. But while the wind is still blowing toward us, we're fine. As long as the direction doesn't change and we don't make any sudden sounds or movements to threaten them, we'll be fine."

"Don't you think we should start running? I mean we have a lion in the bushes!"

"I'd say lionS, actually, as in more than one. Like I said, we're fine for now. We just need to stay low and move in the opposite direction as them. We need to find shelter and preferably before the sun sets fully. I'm more concerned over Jelani. Is he ok?" Alex intentionally changed the topic to direct Sam's attention to more urgent matters at hand.

"I am not sure he's going to make a recovery Alex. Look here," pointing to his stomach as he lifted up Jelani's T-shirt.

"He's got internal injuries for sure. Notice this purple bruising and swelling here. His breathing is also very shallow, and he's lost consciousness. I could be wrong but seems to be his spleen or most likely his liver."

"How do you know all this Quinn? Aren't you an archaeology student with Professor Keating?"

"Well, yes, sort of. It's a long and complicated story. Can you move?" Purposefully moving off topic.

Annoyed with his blatant disregard, Alex managed to get to her feet, albeit still leaning half against the tree and out of sight from the lions.

"Perfect. Do you think you can walk?"

"Yes, I think so, but perhaps we should consider rather climbing this tree, Quinn. I'm just not sure how to help Jelani up there."

"Come on then. We'll take shelter underneath the car wreck for the night and figure something out in the morning. Your head is bleeding again."

Fresh blood drenched Sam's improvised bandage around Alex's head.

"If that is, in fact, lions in the bushes as you suspect, they would beyond a shadow of a doubt smell your blood. I don't think I have to tell you what that means. It is just a matter of time before we are all minced meat."

"Shh, we have to keep quiet." Alex whispered as they watchfully started toward the wreckage.

The upside down four-wheeler lay perpendicular to the ground creating a perfect little cave within the confines of the bull bar and sidebars. With a tiny bit of tweaking, the shelter should do just fine.

"I'll make some fire. The place is abundant with enough dry twigs around to make a big enough fire to keep the lions at bay for the night. I seriously doubt we will be able to sleep much, if any," Alex volunteered while Sam lifted Jelani into the wrecked vehicle.

Alex kept her eyes on the lions. From that angle, she could see two, maybe three female lions and a male lion lying in a circle between the shrubs. They were far enough but still too close for comfort. The sun was almost all the way set which illuminated their golden eyes in the new moonlight. If Alex and Sam wanted to survive the night they'd have to get the fire and shelter going as quickly as they could.

"They seem relaxed for now. I'm not sure if the lions have spotted us yet. Perhaps, if we're lucky, they would have had a full hunt last night," she pacified Sam who was too busy to even think of being prey to a group of lions.

He heard her but didn't react. He had pulled the wreck's doors off and positioned them inside the bars. The rear seat's cushion was flat on the ground, and Jelani lay safely on top. Alex watched as Sam examined Jelani's body with precision. He had one hand flat on Jelani's abdomen while he tapped it with his other hand. Clenched between his teeth was a small flashlight. He checked Jelani's heart rate on the side of his neck and then took the torch and shone back and forth into Jelani's eyes.

"Who are you? Where I come from archaeologists don't carry out medical checkups on the mummies."

Sam ignored her. She cracked another thick branch over her knee and threw the larger one in the fire. She decided to leave him be for now, for Jelani's sake.

The flames burned high and should do the trick but Alex found herself stealing glances at Sam often. With his one sleeve off and his messy hair, he was quite a looker. Tall, dark and handsome. She couldn't remember the last time she noticed a man this way.

Without warning Sam looked up and caught her staring at him with a dreamy look in her eyes. Unprepared and hope-lessly embarrassed, Alex gushed under his warm eyes and quickly busied herself with adding another couple of logs to the fire. She cursed herself for acting like a stupid schoolgirl.

"Is he ok?" Alex asked hoping it would divert his attention from her pathetic behavior.

"I'm afraid not, Alex. He urgently needs a hospital. I suspect he had a serious knock on his head too. If the internal bleeding doesn't stop by itself, he might not make the night. I'm sorry."

"All this is my fault." Alex slumped down against the car.

"Don't be ridiculous. None of this is your fault. I shouted at Jelani to stop the car. But if I am totally honest, the man was driving like a lunatic and was out of control. It was an accident waiting to happen."

But Sam's words did little to shift her guilt and Alex silently cursed her stupid disease. Her head hurt and she had now lost her pills to boot. Her thoughts attacked her mind in a vicious battle over which she had little control.

"Why can't I just pull myself together? My father has gone missing. Jelani is dying, and now I'm stuck in the middle of Africa!"

Sam's hand was suddenly firm on her shoulder, his other hand under her chin tilting her head back. Something in his eyes gave her instant strength.

"We need to clean up your wound, Alex." He pulled out a bottle of sterilizing liquid and a cotton swab from his backpack. The blood had dried up and caused the sleeve-bandage to stick to the wound and Alex pinched her eyes in pain as he pulled it off the open wound.

"Ouch!"

"Sorry. The alcohol might sting a bit, but you need stitches." He dabbed the liquid on the open wound that had started bleeding again.

"I'm going to need you to hold very still Alex. I'm not going to lie. It'll hurt, but I promise to work as quickly as possible."

"No way!" Pushing his hand away. "I am not having you stitch me up. With what, I might ask? Your shoelaces? You're not a doctor last time I checked. We'll be at the hospital in the morning, and I'll ask a proper medical professional to care for me."

"The hospital might not be within our reach by tomorrow, Alex. Look around you. We're in the middle of nowhere with no idea where we are. Your wound is deep, and you can lose a lot of blood by then. Not to mention the fact that, with all this dust floating about, you can easily contract an infection. And no, I have a genuine suture kit. My shoelaces are too dirty," he added a taunting giggle.

The blood trickled down her nose and over her eyes again. She spotted the mischievous twinkle in his eye. He was right, and she knew it. It wasn't as if she had much choice in the matter. Her head wound did seem to be bleeding a lot again and with the lions on the prowl, it might not be safe to leave her injury until tomorrow. They didn't have any idea of where they were. At least not until the sun came up and even then there were no guarantees they'd find their way back.

Sam didn't wait for her to argue again. He held his flashlight between his teeth and tilted her head back, still dabbing at her open wound.

"Okay, fine then. Do what you need to do," she conceded stubbornly.

To her relief, Sam didn't react. Instead, he picked up a stick and placed it sideways in her mouth. Within minutes he had her wound stitched up and dressed with a proper medical bandage from his backpack.

CHAPTER FIVE

The night was a long and a bitterly cold one. The lions continued to prowl around the camp several times during the night but kept their distance as long as the fires were burning high, which was most likely the biggest reason why Alex and Sam didn't sleep much.

"Who knew wood burnt out so fast?" Sam managed to cut the dense atmosphere with one of his let's-lighten-the-mood stints. "I guess we can thank our lucky stars we are in the middle of the bush, can't we?" He added.

His sense of humor in the midst of the direst of circumstances was quite possibly the very reason Alex found herself warm up to her unwanted chaperone. Somehow he always managed to lift her spirits.

At one stage he spread the bonfires into three or four different piles of wood around their camp. It looked as if he almost had fun doing it too.

"Are you a boy scout at heart Sam Quinn?"

"I wish. But I can't lie. I think I might be a pro at this now. Maybe I have a bit of scout in me after all."

Through the night Jelani's breathing became very rapid, and in the early morning hours, he developed a high fever. With the limited water and medical supplies Sam had in his backpack, there was nothing they could do for him out here. Alex stayed by his side throughout the night until she fell asleep somewhere in the early hours of the morning. When she woke she looked across to where he was still lying unconscious. The swelling in his abdomen had doubled in size with bright purple bruising all around it. Sam was already up and checking on him and had done so throughout the night.

"Hey there sleepyhead. How are you feeling?" Sam asked.

"Morning," flashing a slight smile as she sat up. Sudden dizziness threw her off balance, and a sharp, intense pain hit her between her eyes.

"My head hurts, but I'm okay. How's Jelani?"

"Not good I'm afraid Alex. We're going to have to get him to a hospital somehow, urgently. It doesn't look like the bleeding has stopped, and his fever is spiking. Perhaps you want to take a look around now that we have daylight. I don't have any idea where we are."

Alex looked through the opening between the bull bar and the door.

"I can't see the lions."

"Yup. It's been rather quiet for the last hour or so. Let's hope the lions gave up and left for greener pastures."

Sam pushed the rickety door aside for them to get out of their vehicle shelter.

It was daybreak and the sun was just about peeking out behind the now bright orange horizon. Alex looked around across the vast African bush. It was breathtaking. But there was nothing but trees and shrubs for miles in any direction. She wasn't sure how they could have strayed from the road this far into the backcountry. It looked vaguely familiar, but she couldn't be sure. Bush was bush, and trees were trees no matter where you were in the Savannah. There was no way of telling at all. Everything looked the same. She pulled out her map from her backpack in a desperate effort to see if she could make any sense of their location.

"I think we left the road here and possibly veered off over there. We need to head west. If I have my bearings right, we should only be about a mile or two out from the river. If we keep west, with any luck, we should hit the road we were on. If not, we might then at some stage find the river and we can follow it north."

"Right then. We'll have to get a move on quickly before the sun comes up fully. I would hazard a guess that it gets sweltering out here during the day. Fancy a cup of coffee before we leave?"

"Ha-ha, hilarious Mr. Quinn."

She liked a man with a sense of humor. His cunning ability to de-stress the situation was without fail what she needed in that moment.

"Okay, I might have a plan." Sam perked up. "I saw Bear Grylls do this on one of his television episodes once. We need to make a stretcher for Jelani. Let's see if we can find two long branches and something to tie down the car bonnet with on top of it."

"Bear Grylls? Are you serious?" Her giggle didn't throw him.

"What? So I'm a fan, a big one if I may say so. Never miss an episode. Grylls did it and it looked fairly easy. So unless you have a better idea," he remarked with his hands on his hips.

"Oh, I'm not laughing at the idea. Rather just how this adventure has already changed you. I'm just surprised that's all. With your crisp white shirt and shiny shoes, I just didn't peg you for an adventurer at all. And what's with all the medical stuff anyway? How is it that you know more about playing doctor than chasing relics?"

"I read a lot that's all," bending quickly to pick up a nearby branch.

"Nope, I don't believe you Sam Quinn. Reading is one thing, but carrying a full medical kit into the bush and stitching up head wounds is an entirely different thing altogether. I watched you examine Jelani and it seems to me there's an awful lot of medical training there. Call me naive, but somehow I don't suspect it being from watching Bear Grylls episodes."

"It's a long story. Come, the sun is getting higher. We're running out of time."

"Look around Quinn! I've got nothing but time. We are stuck in the African bush with prowling lions, the militia, and who knows what else after us. Spit it out. My life might be at stake, and I deserve to know what I am getting myself into here. Heck, I might not even live until tomorrow."

Sam looked slightly uncomfortable as he tied up the cords from his backpack around his clever piece of engineering. Alex was determined to know the truth. She needed to know whom Professor Keating saddled her with, especially if her life depended on it. Keating said he had been his top student, but it was evident that Sam Quinn had never been on an actual expedition before.

"I'm waiting Mr. Quinn. What's your story?"

"Fine. I'll tell you. I doubt you'll stop until you know anyway. But in the event of us perhaps not seeing another day, and because you're so persistent, I'll give you the short version. As long as you don't judge me. Agreed?"

Alex nodded.

He took a deep breath and continued.

"I'm not exactly an archaeologist. I am in actual fact a qualified trauma surgeon."

"A doctor? What do you mean you're a *doctor*? Professor Keating is head of archaeology and you're supposed to be one of his students so what you're saying now doesn't make sense."

"Hold the knot down there please."

"Quinn! Stop trying to derail the conversation with this stupid stretcher-ma-jig. Will you tell me the truth, please? Who are you? I deserve to know. If anything, at the very least, what I have gotten myself into with you. I mean, do you have any experience with archaeological expeditions or not?"

"Not exactly, this exploration is my first if you must know," sounding sarcastic and annoyed.

Alex swore under her breath.

"These antics are so typical of Professor Keating. I thought you were his 'best student ever.' Of course not. I should have known the moment you sat on that plane with your white-as-snow-shirt and shiny shoes. You are just a pawn in an elaborate plan to get me to go chase after an ancient city that I'm not even sure exists. Not to mention the mysterious key everyone thinks is real. It's a blooming joke. So you're nothing but a babysitter to keep my stupid agora-phobia at bay. You're probably going to get us both killed at some stage too. No wonder Keating insisted I come. It wasn't just a case of finding my father, but finding Rhapta. Sneaky weasel. How could I be so stupid? I'm not some puppet the faculty can use as they see fit. They outright conned me!"

"Are you quite done Miss Hunt?" Sam finally spoke as he pulled tight the last knot of the cord. He stood tall next to her before reaching for Jelani.

"Stop whining and help me get Jelani on the stretcher."

"That's it? You have nothing to say for yourself?"

Alex puffed much like the lions did the night before. She wasn't impressed with how calm Sam was in the midst of her enraged fit but she looked across at Jelani whose fever had spiked out of control, instantly riddled with guilt as she watched him lying there so helpless and innocent in the situation. Jelani didn't think twice about helping her get her father back. He depended on her now. She needed to swallow her pride and focus on getting him to the hospital and fast.

"You lift his feet," she grudgingly spat. She conceded for Jelani and her father. Not because Sam ordered her.

With Jelani safely secured on the make-do gurney, Alex gathered her bag and whatever supplies she could find from the car. There was a small emergency kit and a couple of bottles of water in the cubby and much to her joy, a small compass.

"Hold on Jelani old friend. We'll get you out of here in no time," she whispered next to her injured friend.

With newfound excitement she opened the map and flattened it on the sand, pinpointing the road she suspected they headed out on when they had left the airport. She was right. The river lay to the West, but she had no idea how far along the river the village was.

"I'm going to need to speak to Jelani, Quinn. Will he wake up?"

"No way of knowing right now I'm afraid. We can try."

Alex knelt next to her friend. "Jelani, can you hear me? It's Lakicia."

She waited, but he lay very still.

"Jelani it's me. I need your help to get us home. Can you hear me?"

He groaned the faintest of groans.

"Quinn! He can hear me!"

She tried giving him a sip of water, but he was frail and lay with his eyes still closed.

"Jelani, I'm so sorry. I know you're in pain but I need you to please point out the village on the map. Do you think you can help us?"

She held the map up and lifted his arm, unfolding his limp forefinger and placing it on the river on the map. She watched as her friend forced his eyes open with all the physical strength left in his injured body.

"I got you Jelani. I got you. Help us find our way out of here my friend so we can get you to the hospital."

He moved his hand left, ever so slightly and pointed to a spot by the river.

"It's there? Excellent! Okay, rest my friend. We're going to get us out of here, okay? Just hang in there a little longer."

Alex raised his weak hand gently against her cheek.

"Hang in there, Jelani. Don't give up. Fight!"

"It looks like we are all set then. Let me check your wound and then we can head off," Sam interrupted.

"I'm fine. Let's just get out of here."

"Alex, I need to clean your wound. We can't afford for it to go septic. It's fine if you're upset with me, but Jelani, your father... heck yes, even I depend on you."

"Of course you depend on me. You won't last beyond that bush over there. Just because you made one Bear Grylls experimental thingumabob and a couple of fires doesn't mean you'll find your way to the village. So I guess I'm babysitting YOU, Sam Quinn."

She stormed off in the opposite direction of the sun, noticing Sam had finally changed his clothes. It was screaming never-been-worn-before and she was certain the price tag was still attached, but he looked far more like a relic hunter than a doctor.

"Okay, Alex, please wait? I'm sorry if I told you to stop whining. It was chauvinistic of me."

"You think that's why I'm upset." Alex looked back at Sam where he was dragging the stretcher behind him.

"Well, what then?"

She ignored him not sure why she suddenly had wayward thoughts about how kind he really was. Watching him drag the injured body of a man he had just met, confused her to the point where she herself wasn't even sure why she was angry. It was ridiculous. She had a concussion. That was it. The concussion made her act that way.

"Well, I'm waiting. You're storming off like a bull is chasing you. Do I look like a bull?"

"Oh, so this is funny to you? Well, let's see then shall we? You're a doctor. I asked for an archaeologist, and I landed up with a doctor! Clearly to hold my hand and keep an eye on my stupid condition. What if we never had the accident huh? Would I even have found out?"

"Can you slow down please Alex? I can't keep up. Jelani might be as thin as a stick, but he is nonetheless heavy to haul about on my own. Is this our first fight?"

"First fight. Have you completely lost your mind? Couples fight and last time I checked we are NOT by ANY stretch of the imagination a couple!"

"Ah come on Alex. I'm just playing with you. I'm sorry, okay? Wait. Just stop for a minute, please? Let me explain."

Alex was in her full mind to explain a thing or two to him but decided to stop under the shade of a large thorn tree.

"You deceived me, Quinn. Where I come from it's wrong to lie to people."

"I wasn't telling a lie though Alex, merely not volunteering any information upfront."

"That's hiding the truth. It's the same thing as lying."

"In my defense though, Alex, Professor Keating didn't flat out play open cards with me either, you know? He gave me the assignment, and I took it. No questions asked. The fact that you have an illness was only disclosed to me just before I got onto the plane. Heck, I thought you were a bloke! Besides, I owe him."

"What do you mean 'you owe him'?"

Sam finally caught up with her under the tree. He shuffled restlessly under her questioning gaze; wiping his face before answering.

"I have a very old-school and controlling father okay? I come from a long line of physicians, and he insisted I carry the tradition and pursue a medical profession too. But it isn't my passion in life. Never has been. From as far back as I can remember I've been interested in artifacts and ancient history. I spent hours at the museums. I read every journal there was and by the age of fourteen stumbled upon a National Geographic with your folks on the cover. I was hooked. I knew this was what I wanted to do for the rest of my life and I started following your parents' discoveries all over the world. Becoming a doctor was never on my wish list. Archaeology is down to the core fascinating, but my father didn't want to hear anything about my dreams. It would have placed shame on the sacred family legacy, so I succumbed to his demands. But last year, I lost my best mate in a cycling accident. And suddenly life as I knew it, changed forever."

His demeanor softened as they sat under the shade of the tree, revealing another layer Alex didn't expect to see.

"I realized I was lying to myself, that I am fulfilling someone else's dream and not my own. Life is too short to not go after what your heart desires."

"So you enrolled in archaeology."

"Not quite. My father would disown me. I met Professor Keating at a benefit some time back, and he offered to teach me in the evenings. Night school so to speak, except, it was at his house and one-on-one with one of the country's most respected archaeology professors. In exchange, I would be his wife's physician and see to it that she got the best treatment possible under my supervision."

"Melanie. She died last year of colon cancer. It was awful."

"Yes, Melanie. She fought a good fight right till the end."

Alex caught herself scratching the beginnings of a heart with a stick in the sand in front of her. But she stopped and quickly wiped it clean with her foot.

"And that's it, the whole truth and nothing but the truth. So when your father's situation came up, Keating approached me. I couldn't say no. He's still teaching me at night, even long after his wife passed. Yes, quite possibly because he'd kill two birds with one stone but is that so bad? The guy cares about both you and your father, and I happened to be available and experienced on both levels. Ok fully experienced in the medical field and somewhat experienced in the treasure hunting field, but you get the drift."

Alex was annoyed but somehow Sam always seemed right about everything. So he wasn't perfect and where she lacked he made up for it and vice versa.

"You still have lots to learn about relic hunting, but I suppose you're right. I easily would've done the same, had I been in your shoes. But get this straight Dr. Quinn. I don't do well with liars. No more secrets. If we're going to do this expedition together, we can't be keeping anything from each other. I need to know that you have my back and that I can trust you. I have a sneaky suspicion things could get very messy and out here that means you end up dead."

"Deal," spitting into his hand and holding it out for her to shake.

"Okay, that's pushing it a tad too far. I think you've been in the bush too long. Let's get on with it. We have a long walk ahead of us, and before you know it, the sun will be at its highest."

The next two hours their conversation took on a much lighter tone as they got to know each other. Sam told her about his controlling father and his childhood. How his mother sneaked adventure books into his room. How she managed to sign him up for scouts without his dad ever finding out about it. About his best friend who got hit by an oncoming drunk driver while out cycling and how much he missed him. How the two of them grew up together chasing the same dreams. He shared stories about their regular secret escapades in the nearby woods on an imaginary quest finding make believe hidden treasures and ancient relics. How he was like a brother to him and how his death left a massive void.

Several times through their conversations Alex found herself wanting to hug him and tell him it'll all be okay. Somehow, he had touched the tender side of her and she decided to let him in, just a little.

She found herself pondering how terrible it had to be for him growing up in a home where no one ever supported his dreams. Her parents never once forced her to follow in their footsteps. On the contrary, they tried nudging her out of it. 'Perhaps you should find something safer to do in life. Like a teacher or curator,' her mother always said. Ironically, now that she thought about it, it was the very thing from which her mother ran. Her mother's own parents practically disowned her when she went off on her first expedition. They insisted she become a teacher too, but she defied her father and left on a study group through the university. Good thing it was too. It's where she later met her husband. They seemed to have hit it off from the get-go. Alex recalled how her father insisted they were soulmates even though he didn't really believe in that stuff.

The thought of having a soulmate perplexed her too. Could it be that in the entire universe there was only one person who'd be destined to spend your whole life with you? One soul. Kindred spirits. Thinking the same, finishing each other's sentences, picking from each other's plates.

In her head she concluded that the soulmate theory was just that. A theory.

CHAPTER SIX

3 YEARS AGO - IZZY HUNT

"Charles! Hurry. I think we found something. Look!"

Charles hurried to his wife's side. "Izzy, can it be? Eric hand me the camera. Quick!" He added.

"Be careful Charles. We don't know in what condition it is. Here, perhaps the margin trowel will work better. Careful," she cautioned.

Izzy's breath was caught somewhere between her lungs and her throat. She watched as her husband meticulously scooped away the spoil from what looked to be an ancient weapon.

"Is it a piece of a sword, you think?"

"Hard to be certain at this stage but it looks too short for a sword. Unless the blade broke off or something."

"Ah then maybe a knife? It was one of the most popular weapons back then. Do you realize this could very well be it, Charles? Finally! I mean, if this weapon is from Rhapta then that means it would have to be somewhere here. If we find it, we would be unlocking an immense amount of lost history. A piece of history that the world doomed was buried forever. Do you know what that means?"

Charles Hunt chuckled. "Of course I do Izzy my dear but let's just see first shall we?"

When Izzy first heard about the city that vanished into thin air, she was roughly fifteen years old. She recalled how her father had sat in his chair clicking all sorts of funny sounds with his tongue. He read it in the paper and mumbled inaudible words to himself.

'Sweetheart' he said. 'Perhaps you'll be the one to find the lost treasures one day. Then I can finally go on retirement and take your mother on that boat trip she's always nagging me about.'

Little did he know, that his one single sentence would set Izzy on a course of a life-long adventure. Determined, she made it her quest in life to get them that boat trip. She was so intrigued and fired up she spent hours in her room planning her perfect exploration. Fantasies of climbing through chasms and secret chambers in her quest to find the lost city of Rhapta were her normality. She as much as lived at the library doing copious amounts of research while plotting her course. Now, years on, both her parents have passed away, and she never managed to get them that boat trip they had always dreamed of. She silently wished her father were still alive to see just how close she was to finding Rhapta.

"Well, what do you know?"

Charles sat back, hands on knees and cap in hand staring at the ground.

"Blimey Izzy, it's an ancient weapon indeed. Pinch me. I must be dreaming."

They were at it so long that the excavations almost became mechanical. Like breathing. Something you just do without thinking about it. Day in and day out in the treacherous African sun. None of them ever thought of quitting. They all just kept going in the hope and anticipation that someday... one day... they'd find the lost city of Rhapta.

"We need to keep digging, Charles. If we found a weapon, then we might have hit the spot. There has to be more." Izzy tried to contain her excitement.

"Easy there trooper. You can't rush these things. We have to clean this up very gently. Eric, peg this off but be careful not to step just anywhere."

"Yes sir."

Izzy relished in how Charles always succeeded in keeping her rational. She was one who could charge like an African wildebeest without a second thought of the consequences. He on the other hand seemed to have the patience of Noah when he had to build the ark. There was no way she would have seventy-five years worth of patience in her to complete any task but Charles did. He had been at it since they first met in his final year at uni. Those were her tumultuous years when her father rejected her impulsive decision about her switching majors. Somehow, through the daunting teenage years and breakout parties, she managed to receive a scholarship to Cambridge. Something her father boasted about for years as the first in a line of family members to ever study at a University.

It was love at first sight with Charles. During hazing she was meant to carry his books around and call him 'Master Charles, The Helper of the Cows.' It was a joke playing on the real Charles, Prince of Wales' tribal name given to him during his then recent trip to Tanzania. Quite apt now that she thought of it. As soon as they dipped the corners Charles would take his books from her and carry them in secret. They would sit for hours under the trees in the garden deciphering the myths and new clues found by the earlier researchers in Tanzania.

"We should just do the dig ourselves," he joked one day.

"Sure, I mean why not? If they can do it, we can do it better, right?"

"Indeed Izzy, I feel it in my bones. The two of us will find Rhapta as sure as eagles fly. Together as one team, we will go down in history for the greatest discovery yet!"

And with that, he somehow managed to persuade the Chancellor to sponsor a small group of them to fly to Africa in the hope of making the discovery. It was sure to have the University go down in history for discovering the world's most coveted lost ancient city.

The next couple of years Izzy found herself flying back and forth alongside Charles who, soon after graduating went on to become the uni's top archaeologist. It was kind of unavoidable for Izzy to not go with him on all his expeditions, being his steady girlfriend and all. The girls envied her having the privilege of being by the infamous Charles Hunt's side. Izzy grinned as her mind wandered back.

"And that smile Izzy? What's going through that pretty head of yours?" Charles asked still carefully brushing and cleaning off the relic.

"Oh nothing Charles. I was just thinking back on our journey together."

"And what a journey we've had, my love. But the best is still to come. I can feel it in my bones."

Izzy laughed. "You always say that Charles. But this time, I think my bones agree."

They both sported a laugh so loud and infectious that the excited crew soon laughed with, despite not having the foggiest clue as to why they were laughing. That set Charles and Izzy off into another laughing episode. They always laughed when they were together. It was the one thing they took most pride in with their marriage. Laughter was good. It somehow cleansed their souls of all the sadness that came with them battling to fall pregnant.

Thirty minutes later the relic was fully excavated from the soil and completely unscathed.

"It's a beaut, Izzy! I am almost certain it dates back about eighteen hundred years or so. I can't be sure until we run the tests, but it looks as if it is ivory."

"I would agree with you, Charles. There are striking similarities to it being ivory. I mean it's not impossible knowing that they mainly traded in ivory and tortoiseshell. But see these jagged edges. That must have been hand carved. They would have needed their tools to be able to slice the meat from their hunts—baboon, hippo and so on. Their skins are quite tough."

"You're a walking encyclopedia Izzy, do you know that? I love you!" Smacking a kiss full on her forehead with excitement.

"It's how you got me into all this remember?"

"Ah, you love finding treasures, Izzy. You might have started out researching, but I saw that twinkle in your eyes when we first went to Egypt. You have that hunger in you. Never needed any persuasion from me to go on any of our relic hunts. Excavating is one thing, but chasing! You're a natural my love. You have that instinct no textbook can ever teach you. How many students have you seen come and go huh? They all think they have what it takes. After the fortunes, if you ask me. But, patience, ha! That's the one thing this job of ours tests you at the most. And that daughter of ours, let me tell you. She has it in her too. Chip off the old block."

Izzy smiled with glee. Charles was right of course. She loved chasing after ancient relics. The sheer danger and excitement were enough to make a cat laugh. She missed it most during those days when she finally fell pregnant with Alexandra and couldn't travel much. It was a void she battled to fill with only researching and watching from the sidelines. Not that she would ever give up falling pregnant with Alexandra; not for anything in the world! She was a miracle child after all.

They had battled for many years to fall pregnant; all those doctors' visits and pills and potions in the hope that she would one day fall pregnant. Then, Africa became their solace. Their way of escaping London and the sadness and pressure of wanting a child so desperately. Working hours and hours in complete silence, side by side. Busying themselves with their ongoing quest to find Rhapta. Somehow their Swahili tribe became their family and gave them the much-needed solitude they desperately needed to heal their broken hearts. Perhaps the fact that Izzy couldn't speak much Swahili was a blessing in disguise. Back home it was a constant, 'I'm so sorry Izzy' and 'why don't you just get a puppy or two.' As if!

She found herself looking across their campsite to where an all grown up Alexandra sat working at her laptop. She was fervently at it, eager to acquire as much information as possible on their new discovery. She was nothing but a beautiful blessing to them. A delightful young woman with the same burning fire in her heart. She was worth the wait, that's for sure.

As far as Izzy was concerned time had flown by far too quickly. She remembered so vividly how they had found the first pieces of pottery by the river the very day she realized she was pregnant with Alexandra.

Izzy strolled over to Alexandra and leaned in over her shoulder.

"Find anything yet sweets?"

"Nah, nothing much. At least nothing more than we know already. The first batch of tests should be finished soon, then we should at least know for sure if it is ivory or not. Once that's established it is fair to say it could very well be a Rhapta relic."

"Oh, Alexandra! A relic such as this one is a great find. We are so close I can feel it!"

"Izzy! Come quick. They found something else. Tell Alexandra to bring her computer. We're going to need those fancy programs of hers on this one."

Charles and Eric were hunched over something in the ground when Izzy and Alex joined them.

"What is it?" Izzy asked.

"Not sure my love. In all my years I haven't quite seen anything like it. It is a wooden box of some sort, but there is no opening to a lid or keyhole or latch; nothing, just a piece of wood."

"Hang on. Let me clean it up a bit more. Hand me that small brush, please?"

With a steady hand, Izzy brushed off all the debris and sand while they all watched with bated breath. It didn't take long to get it out of the ground, and a small, rectangular wooden box revealed itself. It was so quiet they could hear cells dividing.

"Hand-carved for certain."

"It would have been ebony wood. They carved anything and everything from ebony and then polished it till it shone. Masks, household items, animals...pretty much anything frankly." Alexandra offered, just beaming with enthusiasm. "See if you can open it though. They used to hide things of value in boxes like these and then buried them."

Talk about an encyclopedia. Alexandra was a born historian. Where she stored all that information only she knew.

"Hmm, this box is a strange one though Alexandra. Look here. I can't seem to find an opening anywhere. I've never seen anything like it. It's solidly closed off on all the sides but there's definitely something loose inside."

"Here, let me see."

Izzy watched as her daughter meticulously inspected the wooden box and minutes later jumped up in elation.

"Do you realize what this is?" She shouted out to Charles like she was opening her presents on Christmas morning.

"It's an ancient puzzle box! Do you know what this MEANS? They only ever put items of significant value in these! Trade secrets, family heirlooms or keys to hidden treasures. I've only read about these and seen pictures of one found in Egypt, but to hold it! I can't wait to tell Jelani."

"Well, can you open it dear? We'd all like to see how this gadget works and if there is, in fact, anything hidden inside."

"It's not that easy Dad. It's most often crafted with extreme precision and has hidden sliders and drawers and latches. It's like a combination to a safe. I have to follow a perfectly executed sequence, or it goes nowhere. Like those Rubix cubes. It can take hours. Days even. Not to mention that it has been buried in the ground for centuries. There's just no way of knowing how long it will take. It might take me a bit, but I'll figure it out."

"I don't doubt that for a minute sweetheart. You're not our daughter for nothing." Charles flashed her a smile.

Over the next couple of hours, they worked the site inch by inch in the hope of finding more relics. Alexandra, on the other hand, ferociously continued at it with the box. A successful day indeed! Two remarkable relics in one day was a spectacular find. Archaeologists can go at it for weeks, months or even years and not find a single artifact.

Izzy looked up at Charles who was grinning from ear to ear.

"You know what's happening here don't you Charles?"

"Oh, I know love. Once Alexandra opens that box we're going to have to start the chase. If it is an old safe as she claims it to be, then chances are there would be a clue in there. Hopefully, one more clue leading us to Rhapta. Let's push another hour before we finish off today, just in case we find one more. It always happens in three's remember? Tomorrow the crew can carry on with the dig, and we can plan whereto from here."

He looked at his wife with a slanted smile while he dusted between the pegs.

"You just can't wait can you?" He laughed. He knew his wife, and he was right. Izzy loved strapping on her boots and crawling through caves.

"You know me too well Charles Benjamin Hunt. I'm running on pure adrenaline right now. How I'm even going to sleep tonight is left to be seen. What's more is that all three of us are together this time. If you think I have ants in my pants, wait until that daughter of ours figures out that box and opens it. She has not put it down once since we found it. It's a matter of time before she cracks it."

"Yes, that daughter of ours is bitten all right and may I just add a walking Wiki-thing."

"You mean Wikipedia."

Charles was old-fashioned and still trying to get acquainted with all the online terminology.

"Exactly, Wikipedia. I have a sneaky feeling we might need to decipher more than just a box though. I can feel it in my bones."

Izzy couldn't help but giggle at his coin phrase again. Somehow, through all the years though, his bones have never lied.

"That's it! I got it! Dad I think I actually got it!" Alex shouted from the tent.

"Are you sure? Open it! Your mother can't bear the suspense." Charles winked at his wife as they joined their daughter in the tent.

Alex slowly pulled back a wedge and flicked up a match-box-sized block that sent off a click and subsequently released the bottom of the box.

The air, thick with anticipation had them all silent as they poised over the box and watched as something dropped out from the drawer onto the table.

"What's that?" Eric spoke for the first time after he had been silently hovering in the background with his camera for days.

"A sort of papyrus scroll I think," Charles answered. "We're going to have to be very careful with this one Alexandra. The paper is quite brittle. Look. There seems to be a seal of some kind on the box."

The question lay heavily on all their minds as they simultaneously looked up at each other. Charles spoke first.

"Bugger that. I say we do it."

"Charles! Have you lost your mind? We can't. It will destroy any value it might hold."

"Where's your sense of adventure Izzy? Come on my love. How long haven't we been at this? Whatever is written on that scroll could lead us directly to Rhapta."

"Or not! We should only open it in the lab Charles. We don't know if the writing is well preserved or not."

"I agree. Open it." Once again, completely out of character, Eric spoke which piqued Charles' suspicions that the guy was acting a little stranger than usual.

"Just saying Boss," Eric excused his behavior and snapped a couple more photos.

"Izzy think about it. If we go at it with care, it should be just fine. We can't leave it now. That makes no sense."

Charles had a point. They have come too far and risked too much.

"Fine. I guess you're right, I suppose. I mean this is what we've been after isn't it? A solid clue or trail to follow," Izzy agreed.

"Open it, Alexandra. Just be careful with the seal. Try slicing it off rather," Charles said eagerly.

With the precision of a brain surgeon, Alex used the scalpel and separated the seal from the paper. It came off with ease and remained intact. She unrolled the yellowed paper scroll and stretched it open.

"Blimey, it's another riddle. Go on, my girl. Read it." Charles exclaimed.

What has a head but never weeps, has a bed but never sleeps, Can run but never walks and has a bank but no money?

"What uncanny twister is this one?" Charles exclaimed in annoyance before having a stab at it. "Has a bed but never sleeps. Perhaps a kind of animal?" he guessed.

"No, that doesn't sound right Charles. Let's just think about this for a second. Running down a mountain... running thin...run short...run fast. Perhaps it is an animal. Like a cheetah or something. They run fast, don't they?"

"No Mum, any animal can walk. See, it says, 'can run but never walk.' Can't be anything with visible legs. Besides, they all have beds too. We're looking at something figuratively. Like running for cover. But then it also says it has a head. It's quite confusing."

"I think you're on the right track Alexandra. It could be parables, nothing literal. We need to think beyond the physical here. No actual objects. '...has a bank but no money...' "

"It's on the tip of my tongue I tell you. I can feel it in my bones, " Charles said before they all bellowed with laughter.

Another hour of deciphering went by before Izzy yelled out. "It's a river!"

"Look! It has a river *head*, a river *bed*, a river *runs* and it has river *banks*. It's a RIVER!"

"Izzy my old darling! See this is why I married you!" He hugged his wife for cracking the riddle.

"Okay great. So we know it's by a river or perhaps in a river but which one? There are a gazillion rivers in Tanzania. We're missing something here. Alex, look for another hidden drawer or something."

"There's nothing Dad. I've looked."

"Where is that seal, Alexandra? Let me have another look at it," said Izzy.

Izzy took the seal from her daughter's gloved hand and inspected it with a magnifying glass.

"It looks like a strange kind of cipher or something, written in Greek, I think."

11525

"A combination perhaps to a lock?" Eric chirped again.

Izzy found herself wondering how Charles found Eric valuable to the team. The uni had insisted they take a photographer for the project for 'publicity sake,' but Eric had been deathly quiet for weeks, never saying a single word. Now all of a sudden he was bubbling with interest. Izzy smelled a rat if ever there was one. She always had a sharp gut instinct. Charles felt it in his bones but Izzy, on the other hand, perpetually sensed when something was wrong in the very pit of her stomach.

"They didn't have combination locks back then, silly. Certainly not like we have them at least." Alexandra spat at him.

"But one thing's for certain," Charles added. "I am convinced we need a key of some sorts. A key that will open up an entire other existence."

CHAPTER SEVEN

ALEX

"We are going to have to find some water soon Quinn. This bottle is our last one."

"How far do you reckon till we get to the river?"

"Not sure, we've been walking for hours, and we're in the heat of the day, which means, what, six hours or so of walking? It could be just on the other side of this tree for all we know, or we could have been walking in circles."

Frustrated, Alex shook the compass and whacked it hard against her palm. She wasn't entirely convinced it even worked.

"I've been following some animal tracks. If we're lucky, it will lead us to the watering hole, and then we can follow

that to the river. The problem is, it could be quite dangerous. Lions aren't the only animals out here you know. We'd
be facing hippos and crocs, and in the muddy banks, the
crocs camouflage themselves completely. We won't neces-
sarily see them until it is too late. That's how they catch
their prey."

As she heard her own voice, fear gripped her insides and
the thought that nighttime was near brought her even less
solace. Most African crocs were nocturnal, so they were
even more alert than during the day. And if the pack of
lions from the previous night were out on the prowl again,
they were as good as dinner.

"It's all a blooming gamble then isn't it?" Sam commented.
"But for now, we're going to have to rest for a bit Alex. I
need to get Jelani in the shade. This heat isn't good for
him."

They slumped down under a nearby tree to rest. The
African bushveld was not a place to hang around for too
long. Usually, the animals spotted someone long before
they even knew of their existence. For all they knew they
were following them already, so sitting still meant they
were open targets.

Jelani's breathing was extremely shallow. Alex used most
of their last bottle of water to wet her hanky in an attempt
to cool his face down a bit. It wasn't any use though. His
fever was out of control. Sam examined his abdomen with

great focus and Alex found herself admiring how he had so much empathy for someone he barely knew and how his glass was always half full. Sam Quinn was the perfect blueprint. But seeing him there, in the middle of the African Savannah in his black T-shirt and matching combat pants, he at least somewhat resembled someone who would have the makings of a great explorer.

"What are you doing?" She asked when he suddenly started cutting up his previously worn jeans and shirt with his knife.

"I'm attempting to make a canopy to keep him in the shade. His fever is dangerously high and this sweltering sun is bound to make it worst."

"So you're cutting up your clothes. How is that going to help?"

He looked over at Alex with a humorous smirk and winked at her.

"Just you wait and see Miss Hunt. I told you. I'm a Bear Grylls fan. Watch and learn."

Alex couldn't help but laugh at him as she waited and observed his invention come to life.

"You know, Alex. You should tune in your telly to an episode or three when we get back. You might learn a thing or two," he joked.

"Yeah, thanks. I cannot sit through even one episode of this man chewing squiggling worms and scorpions with their guts splashing all over the place; not quite my idea of exhilarating. I'll leave this stuff up to you. Speaking of, what's for dinner?"

He doubled over with laughter. She had him in stitches.

"Good one Alex. Even here in the middle of the bush you still have some laughing left in you somewhere."

As for Sam, savvy might just be his middle name, she thought.

"Okay fine. I'll satisfy your craving for commendation. This invention of yours has me just the tiniest bit intrigued," she confessed.

He had plaited his shards of clothing in a crisscross sheet and perched a roof over four sticks to form a square umbrella over Jelani. It was unbelievable she had to admit.

"Intrigued? I'm a blooming genius!"

"Well, I won't go that far, Quinn. But the crisscross does remind me a little of my mum's famous caramel apple pie though."

Alex sorely missed her mum's baked goods and, caught up in the moment, decided to share her memories with Sam. "She wasn't much of a cook and all be told, couldn't care much for preparing meals either, but her baked goods, quite the treat I assure you. The uni faculty went crazy for her pies. Practically fist-fought each other over a slice during the monthly staff meetings." Alex stared out across the vast grasslands as her heart ached for her mother. Everywhere she looked there was something that reminded her of her mother. "One thing is for sure though. Africa is a beautiful continent and my mother wouldn't have wanted to die anywhere else than here," Alex added with a slight giggle as she remembered her dad joking that she had some ancestral roots in Africa because of her frizzy hair.

"What's so funny? This contraption will work I assure you." Sam assumed she was laughing at him.

"Oh, I don't doubt that for a second Mr. Quinn. You're quite something all right."

Their eyes met in that one phrase, and Alex felt warmth turn her stomach inside out before she quickly looked away and blurted out.

"What I mean is that you've got great survival skills. Bear Grylls would be proud."

Alex nervously started pacing around the tree before she made an even bigger fool of herself but Sam luckily didn't comment. He just kept braiding his clothes and before long, pinned a perfect waffled sheet over Jelani. This man somehow surprised Alex again. Jelani was perfectly shaded on a Jeep gurney.

"Do we have any more water?" Sam broke through Alex's thoughts.

"Half a bottle. Here, you can have it. We should last until we reach the river," handing him the last of their water.

He took one tiny sip before wetting her hanky and placing it back on Jelani's head.

"I think this should do the trick for now. Let's crack on Alex. I'm not sure how long he'll be able to hold on. We'll save this last bit for an emergency."

The stranded pair walked west for several more hours without stopping. Spurred on only by their goal to get to the river before sunset. Jelani's condition deteriorated fast and somewhere along the way he had slipped into a coma. The battle started up in Alex's head again. She couldn't believe it had come to this. She wondered how life could be so cruel and was certain she had never felt more helpless in her entire life.

Their individual thoughts and easy conversations kept them going and they learned that their will to survive was stronger than ever. At one stage Alex looked back to check on Sam who was taking significant strain even with her helping him carry the stretcher. Droplets of blood lay in a trail behind the cot. At first, she thought it was Jelani's, but then gathered that the blood was coming from Sam's hands which were bleeding under the strains of the stretcher.

"Quinn, you're bleeding! Stop! Let me have a look."

"Nah I'll be all right. It's just superficial abrasions."

"You can't walk like this. Let me have a look."

She let go on her side of the stretcher forcing him to stop and turned his palms so she could see.

"I'm no medical professional, but it doesn't take a rocket scientist to see that it is more than 'superficial abrasions.' Why didn't you say anything? Here, we can use my shirt to cover the branches, and if you've still got some of the secret stash of bandages in your backpack, we should wrap your hands too."

"You honestly don't have to take your shirt off Alex. It's not that bad, I assure you. Besides, I think it might just be a tad too soon in our relationship."

"Oh, get a hold of yourself, Quinn. I'm not naked under my shirt, you know. I'm wearing a tank. Your hands are bleeding and since you don't have any clothes left beside your pants, we should start using mine."

That mischievous smile of his buckled her knees and melted her insides. He was naughtier than an adolescent teen for sure. She couldn't help but wonder if it meant he was thinking of her in that way. Alex blushed again at the thought of being with him. He was the first man who saw her soul for who she was. He somehow developed an uncanny way of knowing her exact needs. But even though she tried to hide her red cheeks, she knew he had spotted it. The energy between them was electric.

When she was finished wrapping the stretcher's poles with her sleeves, she cleaned and wrapped his blistered hands. "There, that's better. It should do for now, right?"

"I think Bear would be very pleased with our survival skills Miss Hunt, don't you?"

"I think we're a mess, Quinn. We look like we've been through World War II with all our bandages and ripped clothing."

Somehow, in the midst of the African jungle, Alex felt her walls come down one by one. She had been confined and cooped up for so long but Sam Quinn was slowly bringing her soul to life again.

The sun dipped lower towards the horizon as they stopped for another three-minute rest and a quick check on Jelani. They had been heading west for almost eight hours straight, so figured they had to be close to the river.

Jelani gave a dull aching moan.

"Don't move Jelani. Stay still," Sam whispered.

"Is he awake? Jelani, it's Lakicia. Can you hear me?"

Faint groans came from his weak body, but he kept his eyes shut. He looked gray, although Alex wasn't sure if it was from the dust kicking up or from his injuries.

"What's going on, Quinn? Is he all right?"

Sam ignored her. He had his torchlight in Jelani's eyes and then lightly tapped on Jelani's tummy again.

"Quinn! Is he okay?"

Blood trickled from Jelani's nose and mouth as Alex and Sam watched.

"That doesn't look right, Quinn. Do something." Alex pleaded.

Her voice was no more than a faint whisper, and her hands trembled as she battled to control the flood of emotions that overcame her. She knelt down next to Jelani and wiped his mouth with her hand. Somehow, even though she had no medical training whatsoever, she knew this was his end. She looked up at Sam where he had squatted on the opposite side. He did nothing but look at her with apologetic eyes. Tears pooled in her eyes, but she forced herself not to show Jelani any weakness.

"Don't worry Jelani. You are a warrior. I'm here my friend. Right by your side. You're the best friend I have ever had. I'll take care of you."

She got up abruptly and moved to the front of the stretcher.

"Come Quinn. Hurry! We need to get him to the village."

But before Sam could take his position behind the stretcher, they heard a final groan, and the most silent of breaths left Jelani's body.

Aptly, at that very instant, Alex and Sam heard the thunder bellow from the gray clouds above their heads and droplets of rain gently fell down on them.

Mere days ago Alex stared out through her window wishing she could have the courage to go out into the rain again, and here she was. But it wasnt anything she remembered it to be.

She dropped the stretcher and stared down at Jelani's lifeless body.

"No! Jelani you can't die. Wake up, Jelani, wake up!"

But he was gone. She fell to her knees and pressed her ear to his chest. "Wake up Jelani, wake up please?"

Self-blame engulfed her once again as she cursed herself for causing the commotion in the car that had him crashing into a tree. In that moment she blamed herself for letting them take her mother all those years ago and now allowing her father to chase after her memory and putting Jelani in this position. As she sat frozen in time, staring down at Jelani's lifeless body, the heavens declared their mighty power over the earth and she vaguely became aware of Sam's hand over hers.

"I'm so sorry Alex. There was nothing more I could do for him."

Sam's words made her angry. She didn't want to hear the typical script all doctors used when a patient under their care died. How they got away with it was ill understood by her. Nothing anyone said in that moment of loss could ever make it better. She was numb except for the sudden uncontrollable angst that trapped her breath in her throat and constricted her. What if she never made it out of there alive? She could die there too. Just like Jelani and her mother and probably her father as well. Eaten by lions or gored by a rhino, right there in the middle of the African bush.

"Alex look at me."

Sam's hands gripped her shoulders as he tried to force her to look at him. But all she felt was her body shaking uncontrollably and her breath still caught in her throat. She couldn't seem to get any oxygen into her lungs. It was stuck, wedged in her throat with nowhere to go.

"Alex, I'm going to inject you with Diazepam. Just a little to calm you down."

Seconds later the sharp sting of the needle pierced her dehydrated skin. Not even when Sam's strong arms pulled her under the shelter of the tree next to him, did Alex react. The drugs didn't take long to kick in, and Alex found herself going through the same lightweight sensation she had back at her apartment in London. Though her body felt numb, her heart still ached inside her chest as she mourned her friend's death.

"Relax Alex. You'll be fine. I've got you," Sam whispered next to her ear.

He deliberately had her back towards Jelani's dead body on the ground and when she fought to have another look just to be sure it wasn't all a dream, he firmed his grip on her.

"All right GI Jane, just relax. You don't want that image etched in your mind, trust me. Focus on breathing deep slow breaths instead."

The man always had to be right, and she couldn't stand it. But she found herself adhering to his breathing prompts nevertheless.

"In... and out. In...and out. Keep going. In...and out."

The steady inhaling and exhaling helped, and soon she breathed normally again. The rain was wet and cold on her skin. In the midst of her breathing ritual, he took the shade-net structure off Jelani's stretcher and positioned it over them.

"That should do it. You're okay now Alex. Just relax. The meds had a stronger effect than I anticipated. I assume because you haven't eaten in days."

She watched as he gently tipped Jelani off the stretcher and wedged the steel plate against the tree sheltering them from the rain. From his backpack he took out a couple of dry twigs and bark and before she knew it, he had kindled a fire underneath their shelter. With skill he broke more branches that were still relatively dry from the tree above them. The crackling sound and the heat from the fire lulled her body into a peaceful sleep.

The rain soon stopped, and the full moon sat high above the dark clouds, casting an organic torch-light across the Savannah. The night was eerily silent. In London the city noises were often deafening, but at least a sign of life. Out there the intense silence thud in their ears. As the night grew colder they sat tightly together in a futile attempt to keep warm. The climate in that part of Africa was one of being sweltering hot during the day and adversely freezing at night. When Alex got up in the deep hours of the night to gather more wood for the fire, she stopped dead in her tracks when she came face to face with a lioness about thirty meters away.

"Quinn," she said in a muted monotone.

"Get up slowly and bring a fire torch with you. We have company."

He had been resting his head against the tree when she got up. With her back toward him, there was no way of knowing if Sam had even heard her. Her eyes stayed fixed on the lioness. She knew full well that, if she dared look away, the lion would charge. So Alex tried getting Sam's attention again.

"Quinn, can you hear me? Bring the fire torch."

"What?" He jerked up from a deep sleep—not impossible at all considering it was his first sleep since the accident.

"Shh," Alex cautioned, but it was too late. The lion had already spotted Sam and they watched as the lioness pulled back her upper lip exposing her white fangs. She was down in an attacking position and ready to charge at anything that moved.

"Quinn, no sudden moves. Reach over slowly and grab the fire torch. Don't make hasty moves. This lion is ready to charge."

Alex knew that if there was one female lion, there was guaranteed to be a pack of hungry males lying in wait behind her. Aware of Sam taking his time in coming up behind her with hopefully a torch in hand, Alex cautiously moved back toward the tree.

"Can you climb a tree, Quinn?"

"Do I have a choice?"

"Pass me the torch, slowly."

Alex gripped the burning branch, her eyes still firmly fixed on the prowling lion. Her suspicions were correct. The fire illuminated the grass ahead, and about five pairs of glowing eyeballs glared back at her.

"Now step back slowly and climb the tree from the other side."

She was sure she could hear Sam's heart beating or perhaps it was hers.

"Now's not the time to be dragging your feet, Quinn."

She still felt dizzy. The drugs hadn't worn off yet which ironically kept her wits about her. She was far calmer than she ought to have been.

"Hurry Quinn. I'm only going to have a split second to climb that tree before these beasts charge for me."

"Okay, I'm up. How high should I climb, though? I mean, don't lions climb trees?"

"As high as you can go Quinn. Hurry!"

She kept eye contact with the lion and slowly took small steps backward toward the tree until her back hit the trunk.

"Can you break another branch off and lean lower so I can light it with my torch? I'm going to have to drop this torch if I want to beat the lion up the tree."

The males seemed to get impatient with their female hunter and chuffed a couple of murmured growls at her. It was enough to have her take a step forward. It wasn't the time for Alex to hesitate. She needed to get in that tree before the lion killed her.

"I got you Alex. Come!"

Alex cast her torch at the lion and, like a bullet leaving its barrel, she climbed the tree faster than she had ever thought possible. Assisted by Sam's firm hand, she made it through the thorny branches just in time.

The lion and two other females she never knew were there, charged straight toward them. One's massive paws were halfway up the tree trunk, ducking at the flailing torch. The others thankfully backed off for some bizarre reason.

Safely up in the tree, perched like a sprawling eagle, Alex picked up a commotion between the male lions on the ground. It took her several seconds to register that they had pounced on Jelani's corpse that lay under the tree.

"Jelani! No! Get away you beasts! Leave him alone!"

But it was too late and Alex and Sam watched as the pack of carnivores dragged Jelani into the darkness of the night. "NO!"

Alex quietly prayed that it was just a horrific nightmare and that she'd be waking up in her bed any minute.

"This just can't be happening, Quinn. There's no way I would be in Africa in the middle of the bush watching a pack of lions devour my childhood friend. Tell me it's not true."

"I'm so sorry Alex," Sam repeated next to her, but she ignored him.

Because if he was indeed speaking and next to her in that tree, it meant she wasn't asleep and that horrible ordeal was very, very real.

CHAPTER EIGHT

3 YEARS AGO - IZZY

They were all up early that following morning. The excitement of their most recent discoveries injected an invisible surge of energy amongst the crew. It was the closest they came yet to finding anything worthy that showed significant evidence that Rhapta did exist. They had tangible proof that they could very well be extremely close to finally discovering the lost city.

"Has anyone seen Eric this morning?"

Charles was frantically running about camp looking for Eric. Something he did only when he got flustered and was under severe stress.

"What's the hullabaloo about Charles? I'm sure he's somewhere."

"I need the photos to submit our findings to the university. They want it yesterday."

Charles was an overachiever of note.

"You are such a perfectionist, Charles. I'm sure they're not that urgent for it."

"No Izzy, it's vital we send it right away. This is where we have to set aside patience and deliver."

"What exactly are you in such a tizzy over, Charles?"

He ignored Izzy and stomped off, irritated with her nonchalant attitude.

It took a unique character to show enough patience to dig for hours on end for something he didn't even know existed. 'Fairytales and unicorns' was how her father always put it and yet, there they were staring back at her from the table.

They found a primal knife made from ivory, an ancient scroll in a never-been-seen-before cryptogram wooden safe and now a cipher code in Greek. Three steps closer to finding Rhapta.

"Izzy," Charles came barging into the tent again. "That chap has disappeared, camera and all. Where on earth could he be?"

"I'm sure I saw him at first light when I got up. He must be here somewhere. Have you checked all of the vehicles

Charles? As far as I know, he doesn't like sleeping in the tents; something about the rhinos coming for him at night. Don't ask. The crew have been teasing him about it ever since he confessed it around the fire the other night."

"Well, the fool has vanished off the blessed earth. I can't find him anywhere and the uni is on my back for the photos. Some high society benefactor is due to arrive today, and they're trying to squeeze more money out of the guy. So they need proof we are telling the truth and have found enough to continue the dig."

Charles took off his hat and wiped his brow. "We can't afford losing this, Izzy. The uni took a bit of strain after the last hazing debacle hit every British newspaper. The ramifications of it caused some of the elite sponsors to cease their donations in support of the stop-hazing campaign. We need this."

Charles stopped and took a large swig of whiskey to calm his mood before moving over to where Alexandra was still at it with her computer and the fancy cipher code. It was probably the only way to distract him right now, so Izzy followed him.

"What time do you want to leave Charles?"

He didn't answer her, decidedly deep in thought as Alex and he worked through the cipher using all sorts of decryption tools on her computer.

"Charles, I said, what time should we leave in the morning? We're going to have to get an early start. I've been working on the map, and the river it's most likely to be is the one out here. Look," pointing to the map spread open on the table.

"Sure Izzy." Charles was engrossed with the cipher code. Ordinarily, most wives would get utterly annoyed at his blatant pass-over, but Izzy just laughed. She knew there was nothing on this earth that could take Charles Hunt's attention away from the cipher now. It was best just to let him get on with it in his own way until he cooled down or wore out, whichever came first. So Izzy turned her attention back to the map and started plotting out a couple of options for them to take.

"My golly Alexandra, you are indeed something special. I can't believe it. You definitely got my brains my girl!" Charles bellowed a laugh.

"Izzy, I think our genius child got it again!"

Alex was something all right and Izzy never grew tired of her daughter's brilliance.

"You never cease to surprise me, Alexandra. Show me."

Alex pointed to several Greek numbers on her computer screen.

"See Mum, I think it's no more than pointing to a particular letter of the alphabet. But, back then everyone used the

Roman or Greek alphabets only. The English language was rarely spoken and only by dignitaries from England. So most secret presidential communications were done in another language, like French or Portuguese. So, hiding something would have had to be somewhere far less obvious to the general population at the time. It was hands down genius. They used the English alphabet instead. They wrote the numerics in Greek, but the cipher is, as a matter of fact, English. Look. Eleven is the eleventh letter of the alphabet which in our English alphabet is the letter K. Five is the fifth letter of the alphabet which is E. Twenty-five is the twenty-fifth letter which is Y. See?"

"So that spells K-E-Y... key!" Izzy proclaimed a tad too loud.

"Yes, KEY," Charles echoed jubilantly. "That's just brilliant. Now, if it is, in fact, a physical key or perhaps rather a kind of solution to a problem, we don't know yet. But I reckon we are getting closer by the day Izzy. I told you it happens in three's. We are so close. Have you managed to come up with anything from the river clue?"

"I think so. I mean I can only think it is the river where we found the first pieces of pottery. Remember? The one that is close to Mafia Island. Legend has it that Rhapta was in that vicinity, so it makes logical sense to try there first, right? It's not a very long river so we should be able to work it easily. My best guess is we should start at the mouth and work it upwards. Chances are the river would have brought any artifacts down towards the mouth in any event. We would have to leave early in the morning though. It is quite a drive there."

Charles shifted his weight uncomfortably as if he was getting ready to dance the shuffle.

"Okay. What's up? I know that look on your face Charles Benjamin Hunt."

He cleared his throat, removed his hat again and scratched his head as if he was trying to gather the words for an announcement at a funeral.

"What is it, Charles? Spit it out," Izzy urged.

"Izzy, I spoke to the uni earlier. You know, brought them up to speed on what we have found. They... well... they need me back home."

"What do you mean? You're leaving us?"

"My love, I have no choice. If I don't go, they will pull all our funding. We are so close now and we cannot afford them pulling the plug now. We have to push forward now more than ever."

Izzy crossed her arms like a spoiled child. She wasn't pleased in the slightest and that would be putting it mildly.

"Oh, come on Izzy. Don't pull the sulking card, my love. You know I would much rather hunt this down with the two of you. My hands are tied. Don't be mad, please?" He attempted to hug his wife but she shrugged him off.

"We are on the cusp of, without a doubt the continent's biggest find ever. Our first proper breakthrough at finally finding Rhapta after decades of digging and now you choose to leave? Really?"

Disappointment couldn't describe how Izzy felt. As if someone just spoiled a surprise.

"When are you leaving then?" She eventually asked.

"First light."

"Great! So at the peak of us finding Rhapta you, the head of this team, are leaving. I can't believe you, Charles! Please tell me it's a joke? How on earth am I supposed to do this on my own?"

"But you are not on your own Izzy. Alexandra is very capable of doing this with you. In fact, I bet my life's savings that she'd be far more worth to you going forward than me. She has learned from the best, haven't you my darling girl?" He winked at his daughter.

"Don't bring Alexandra into this Charles. It might not even be safe for us out here on our own. Once word gets out that we are onto something every rival gang and wannabe treasure hunter will be on our heels."

"I have already thought of that and taken care of that for you Izzy. The chief is assembling a crew to accompany you, and Jelani is in charge. His name doesn't mean "mighty" for nothing. You will be in good hands I'm certain. We will all leave together on my way to the airport tomorrow morning, okay?"

His pacifying hardly brought his wife solace. Quite the contrary if truth were told.

"But Charles, what if we do find Rhapta, finally after all these years of looking for it together. You won't be with us to share in it. That's what I am furious about."

Charles pulled his wife into his arms.

"You'll be okay Izzy. I'll be with you in spirit, and Alexandra... well, let's just say I am certain she will be filling my spot just fine. As soon as you find it you let me know, okay? I'll be on the first plane in."

"Mum, it will be okay. I will be there with you every step of the way and, thanks to technology, we will Skype and take some pictures and send it to Dad, okay? It will feel like he is right here with us."

"Speaking of pictures. Eric is still missing. He had better crawl out from wherever he is before we leave. I need to take those pictures and data with me."

Izzy looked around. She too found it strange that he'd disappear like that in the middle of all the action.

. . .

W ith their belongings packed and the recently discovered relics firmly tucked into her bag, Izzy and Alex set off later in the afternoon to their Swahili tribe by the river. Halfway down the dirt road, convinced someone was following them, Izzy looked back, but the dust clouds behind them were too thick for her to have a clear view. She had a bad feeling about this. She couldn't quite put her finger on it though but something just didn't feel right. Charles looked perplexed also. Perhaps he was sensing it too or most likely, his mind was long since at the benefit back home and his thoughts were all about how to save their expedition. They followed the strict instructions sent to them by the chief and veered off the road at a certain point. Once they got to their marker, they were to do the rest on foot, heading west where the tribe would meet up with them and take them into their village. It was a reasonably normal security procedure. There were many rival tribes in Tanzania, and they needed a handful of precautionary measures to protect their settlements from one another.

When they finally arrived at the marked spot, they walked an hour or so into the bush. Soon after, they heard their tribal call from a nearby Acacia tree and Charles answered back with the same whistling sound by holding his hands clenched over his mouth. Izzy never really got the technique right to mimic their call. Somehow both Alexandra and Charles had managed to learn the secret call. Charles always said it was because her hands were so dainty and small.

Izzy still couldn't shake the feeling that someone was watching them. She turned once more to see, but there was still no one there. Just vast open grassland and a couple of giraffe about a hundred yards away. Most of their crew stayed behind at camp continuing the excavation which now left their small party entirely exposed. Doubts if the one rifle Charles had slung over his shoulder was sufficient filled her mind. Maybe that was why she was restless, she thought.

Another hour on foot led by the tribe's tracker had them reach the river. After months in the barren Savannah, being right next to a river was sheer bliss. A remedy for her soul, she always said. There was something about flowing water that washed all her troubles away.

Jelani came running over to Alexandra, or rather, as the tribe affectionately called her, Lakicia, which translated to 'she who is a favorite among people'. They honored her with a Swahili name shortly after Charles and Izzy took Jelani in. Being the Chief's son, he saw her as his tribal sister, and they held a large ceremony in her honor. He was about ten years her senior and they got on remarkably well. Growing up an only child, she thought of him as her older brother. Jelani naturally took it upon himself to look after her while Charles and Izzy were often away on dangerous expeditions all over the world, forced to leave Alex behind. Izzy's heart warmed at the thought of how it literally took a village to raise her.

The tribe welcomed them with song and cheer when they approached the village. It was the old familiar welcome they got each time they left on an exploration when they gifted them with food and supplies. And each time they came back, they lay a carpet of fresh flowers and leaves out before them and held a welcome celebration until late at night. It was good to see them all again, Izzy thought. Most of them had become dear friends. With Charles and her off on explorations for months on end they never really managed to root anywhere, much less make any friends; acquaintances on the other hand were plenty.

Back in London it was more fame than friendship. Everyone wanted to know the famous Hunt chasers—as they were dubbed. They practically bowed before them at the uni. The students usually lined up outside Charles's office with some or other frivolous excuse just to see him. He loved it though. History and archaeology were in his veins. He could entertain the students with his relic hunting stories for hours on end and reveled in it.

But for Izzy, being out there in the open African Savanah filled her spirit and as they walked toward the fire pit in the center of the village several young ones came running toward them. Some of the girls made beautiful flower hairbands, and forced Alex and Izzy to sit patiently while they decorated their hair accompanied by giddy giggles. This tribe was as close to family as they'd ever have.

A little one tugged at Izzy's pants and she bent down to say hello.

"And who might you be little one?" Izzy asked.

The girl was too young to talk. About two and a bit if one might hazard a guess.

"Hello, Ma'Izzy,"Jelani's voice came up behind her.

"Jelani my boy, how are you?" Hugging him like he was her very own. He had always called her Ma, short for mama. He was still so young when his mum died that it came quite naturally to him, and Izzy didn't mind.

"Very well Ma'Izzy. Meet our Imani. She's my little girl. The gods have blessed me. You are a big mama now."

Izzy's heart skipped several beats as she scooped the little girl up into her arms. That meant she was a grandmother. Never in her wildest dreams did she ever think she'd ever be as fortunate to be a grandmother. Albeit not a blood related one like she'd be to Alexandra's kids. If she was ever going to get married and have one was a question for another day. Alex never held down any boyfriends much. She always had a reason for it not working out but Izzy realized very early on she was just scared of getting hurt.

"Jelani, she is utterly gorgeous. With a name meaning 'faith' you named her well."

"She reminded me of you Ma'Izzy, when you couldn't make a baby, before Lakicia. You always said when life got you down you just need a little faith, remember?"

He was right. She always had faith.

"Well, Imani let's see if I can remember the song I used to sing to Alexandra when she was your age. You want to sing a song with me?"

> Twinkle, twinkle little star
> How I wonder what you are
> Up above the world so high
> Like a diamond in the sky
> Twinkle, twinkle little star
> How I wonder what you are

Seeing the little girl made Izzy happier than she thought ever possible. She never thought she would have her own baby let alone a grandchild.

Alexandra watched from a distance, as if the toddler might bite her. Izzy giggled and held the toddler out to her.

"No thanks, Mum. Babies don't like me."

"Don't be silly Alexandra. Try. She won't bite. Well, maybe just a little," she teased.

"Yeah, thanks, Mum. I'll pass. My hands aren't clean anyway. Sorry, Jelani, no offense."

"When are you taking a husband, Lakicia? Imani will need a play friend, and you are not getting any younger."

"Oh no, I'm leaving that to you, my friend. I am not planning on ever getting married. Men are just trouble. You go ahead without me and string in as many as you wish. I'll sit this one out."

Charles came up from behind.

"What do you mean we're trouble? I would watch my mouth if I were you sweetheart. Look around you. Half the villagers are men," Charles resounded into another belly bout of laughter.

L ater around the fire, Charles and Izzy sat gazing at the stars in silence. Something they had always liked to do. Being out under the stars always bonded them together somehow. Like the heavens held an invisible blanket over them. A quilt only the two of them shared. It was their way of uniting as one.

"What a beautiful night huh Izzy? I mean, you and I have been all over the world to some pretty amazing places. But where in the world are the stars brighter than right here in Africa?"

"You're right Charles. Somehow the air is much cleaner out here too. I could live here you know."

"Well, tell you what my love. Find Rhapta for us tomorrow, and we very well could spend the rest of our days together here under the stars. Perhaps we can finally build that house we have always dreamed of. I know the Chief would gladly help. Right there on the hill overlooking the river. I'll build it on stilts. Safely off the ground, especially for you my love."

"You are such a sweet soul, Charles. I knew the day I met you that you were my soulmate. The one I am meant to be with all of my days."

There was nothing Charles wouldn't do for Alexandra and Izzy. One thing was clear. Izzy knew, with all her heart, that he would much rather stay behind and be with them than fly back to London arguing over money with the snooty benefactors.

Instantly she regretted her outburst that morning.

"Make sure you hurry back okay, Charles? It might take us days before we find Rhapta."

"It's not up to me Izzy darling, but I'll try. I promise."

"Well, if you hurry it along you would have enough time to go home, finish whatever those stiffs want from you and come straight back to make our discovery with us, right here where you belong."

"I would love nothing more Izzy. I think you are going to be successful tomorrow. You are going to somehow find the right spot by the river and figure out where or what the KEY is. You, Izzy Hunt, are going to find Rhapta, my love. I can feel it in my bones."

CHAPTER NINE

ALEX

The shrill shrieking sound of a Hadeda flying circles above their thorn tree woke them. Alex despised those birds. It was quite possibly the single most annoying, shrieking sound she had ever heard. It was enough to set anyone off to a bad start on any day. She looked down at where several Hadeda's and a couple of vultures wrestled over Jelani's remains that were left by the lions' attack the night before. It was nauseating to watch knowing that it was an ill-deserving human they were fighting over. Alex was still in denial over his death. Jelani always protected her and now, she failed hopelessly in protecting him. The only genuine friend she'd ever had, and she failed him miserably. She had no idea how she was supposed to tell his father what had happened.

The thorny branches from the tree left her legs achy and sore to the point where she couldn't feel her coccyx anymore. The sun was just about up and cast a bright orange backdrop against the horizon. Stiff body and all, she got into a standing position to stretch and take it all in. In light of her sorrow and anguish the landscape was surpassingly beautiful and considering the circumstances, she somehow managed to get a couple of hours sleep.

But her head still hurt. And then, while her thoughts trailed and the sun rose higher, her eyes settled beyond the dry grasslands.

"Quinn! Wake up! I see it! The river, I see it!"

She climbed higher in the tree just to be certain her eyes weren't deceiving her. After all, she was severely dehydrated and still woozy from her meds but this was no mirage or hallucination.

"Quinn! Get up!"

How Sam managed to sleep so soundly on a branch filled with thorns was beyond her, so she called again, poking his shoulder with her foot.

"QUINN!"

"What's the commotion about Alex? I usually like my cup of coffee first."

"So funny Quinn, look, there's the river! I can't believe it. We are just about there. We couldn't be closer. How could this have happened, Quinn? We should have walked faster yesterday then... perhaps Jelani might have still been alive."

Alex cried for the first time since the incident. She never cried, ever. Crying was a weakness and she didn't like bearing her soul. But right there, in the moment of exhaustion and hopelessness, years of buried emotions and heartache soaked the earth below as her tears kept flowing. The stress of having left her home, facing her disease and going after her father who was still missing, topped by the death of her dearest friend, was entirely too much for her to keep inside.

Quinn got up behind her, and, for the first time, Alex noted the scratches all over his face. They had to climb the tree so quickly to escape the lions that the hazardous thorns were the last thing on their minds.

"I'm so sorry Alex. I know he meant a lot to you but please rest in knowing that Jelani's injuries were quite severe. Even if we had gotten him to a hospital or the village for that matter immediately after the accident, he might not have made it either way. He had excessive internal bleeding."

"But at least his father and the tribe could have said their goodbyes and they would have had a body to bury. That, right over there by the river, is his village. I cannot believe how close we are, Quinn. Now, I have to go there with not only the sad news that he is never coming back, but also somehow explain where his body is. How do I tell his father that lions devoured his son? And that it happened as much as in their back yard. It is simply too sickening for words."

"Alex I'll help you, okay? Delivering bad tidings to a family is something I've done many times before. It's not my first time. Trust me, I've had my fair share. It will be okay, I promise."

His comment enticed her to react but instead she suppressed the urge to throw a rock at him. How could anything make it okay? It will never be okay.

"Do you think the lions are gone or are they still hanging about?" He asked, already moving on from the topic.

She had no more fight left in her. Alex wiped her eyes and searched the bushes for the lions or signs of any other predators lurking about.

"I can't see any. It is possible the animals left for the watering hole already after they had their fill last night."

Even saying it repulsed her.

"Do you think it is safe for us to climb down then?" Quinn asked, desperate to distract her from her thoughts.

"Well, it isn't as if we have a choice in the matter, do we? We have to take the risk and hope for the best."

"Come on then. Let's get down. It doesn't seem that far so let's get on with it. I don't think I can last another night in a tree."

But Alex couldn't let go of the fact that she had to give the bad news to the village when they got there. Sam's words were little consolation. This was not one of his patients whom he'd never see again. African tribes took death very seriously and empty words weren't going to be enough.

The Chief will insist on knowing the truth and Alex knew the truth would not be easy to convey. Especially when she hadn't come to terms with it herself yet either. There was no sugar coating it. She'd have to tell it as it was.

Riled up with the monologue in her head, she jumped the last bit from the tree and almost landed on what looked like a piece of Jelani's leg. The bile pushed up into her throat. If she had a full meal in her stomach it would have been out already. Lions were once majestic creatures to her. Not anymore. She stormed off in the direction of the river not looking to see if Sam was behind her. She just needed to get out of there. All she felt in that moment was anger. And a bucket load of guilt.

She dealt with her emotions far better in solitude. Locked up at her home. It was easier to sweep it under the rug and lock it down forever. She didn't want a stranger around her and she didn't want to deal with this. But deep down, she realized, much to her dismay, that her life was nothing like it was before. Everything had changed.

"Hey, Alex, wait up!"

She slowed down just enough to see that Sam was still trying to get down from the tree. He somehow managed to get himself stuck in the thorns. She was so absorbed with herself that she didn't even think he might be dealing with life too. She knew it wasn't his fault. He had been nothing but kind and supportive from the moment they met. In that moment, she discovered that Sam Quinn was the very definition of a true friend.

"Go easy on me, Alex. If you haven't gathered, I'm not exactly the Bear Grylls kind. Have you forgotten you also still have a head wound and by now, you are bound to be severely dehydrated on top of it. Let's just take a slow and steady walk okay?"

He always placed her needs ahead of his. The fact that he was bleeding from the thorn scratches on his head wasn't even a consideration for him. As long as she was okay then all was dandy.

And he was right. Again, of course. She was in fact a little dizzy, and she did need to take it easy.

As the Savannah glowed under the orange sunrise, Alex and Sam walked in silence. Her medical bracelet glistened in the morning sun. Alex Hunt - Agoraphobic. It didn't ring true anymore.

Something had changed right there in the African Savannah.

"I think you have come a long way with your disease, Alex. Fine, your emotions are a bit volatile still but look at yourself. You are out here in the open grassland in the middle of Africa. You fought off lions. Twice! If that doesn't say everything about your inner strength to overcome, then I don't know what will."

Sam's words surprised her. He always knew exactly what she was thinking. How that was possible she didn't know, but she wasn't sure she wanted him inside her head. She ignored his praise and instead, changed the topic.

"We should be there in about twenty minutes or so. It's an easy walk."

It wasn't long before Alex heard the tribal whistle from a nearby tree. She recognized it in an instant and just about jumped for joy. With her hands clenched and positioned in front of her mouth, she answered back with the same whistle indicating that they were friendlies. Sam's admiration for her skill made her smile within. She felt empowered and silently vowed she would let him in, just a little. There was a whole lot about the real her he didn't know yet.

. . .

A watchman startled them as he jumped out from a tree about five meters in front of them. Alex didn't recognize him but she answered him in Swahili and followed him to the village.

It was great to be back in the village again. Within minutes women and children surrounded them, and Alex rejoiced in seeing a few familiar faces. They had made it. But when the welcoming committee settled down, reality of her father's kidnapping was evident. A number of the bomas were burnt to the ground and under repair by the women. There was enough evidence of the callus attack by the rebels and the damage they had done. Burning the tribal houses was undeniably part of the plan to warn them about whom they were dealing with and that they had meant war.

From the corner of her eye, Alex spotted Jelani's father who was in hot pursuit to welcome them home.

"Lakicia, welcome my child. We expected you days ago. It has been too long since we have had the pleasure of welcoming you back in our village. I'm sorry it is not under more pleasant circumstances but my men will not stop until we find your father."

Alex felt the familiar constricting feeling around her throat knowing the chief had no idea just how dire the circumstances really were. Her father, at least, God willing, was still alive somewhere, unlike his son. The man had grieved the loss of his wife already and now his only son would never return to him again.

His firm embrace provided little comfort as Alex dreaded giving him the news.

"Come Lakicia. You need water and food." The chief signaled to some of the women who hurriedly set out clay jugs of fresh water and a display of fresh fruit in front of them.

"Are you okay? What happened to you? Jelani left days ago to fetch you at the airport. I don't understand. Did you not find him waiting for you?"

It was only then that the chief paused to size Sam up and down and Alex found great relief in the opportunity to delay her answer to his question.

"Forgive me chief," she said as she swallowed a large chunk of sweet melon halfway through her sentence to buy even more time. She was sick to her stomach and not much in the mood to eat, but the fruit was a welcome excuse to occupy her mouth and prevent her from having to speak.

"This is Sam Quinn. He is from the University. He has come to help me find my father."

And babysit, she added in her head.

"Welcome to our village Sam Quinn."

The chief's blank expression hinted what was to come next as his eyes searched the village for Jelani.

Alex, on the other hand, searched Sam's eyes, silently pleading for a way out. Regardless of how hard she tried, she simply couldn't get the words out and forced another piece of fruit down instead. It was inevitable though. She had to say what needed to be said.

"Chief, uhh... ahem...I'm afraid I have some devastating news," she stumbled through. In her mind she cursed Sam for not jumping in and come to her aid as he had promised.

The chief's eyes held hers firmly. As if he already knew the very thing she was about to say, but he didn't flinch nor speak. He just sat there, hands on knees, waiting for Alex to talk. She was convinced he was mentally preparing himself in advance for what was to come as she bit at her thumbnail and tried again.

"I... ahem...Jelani... well..."

Desperate she searched her mind for the right words to tell the Chief that his only son was devoured and ripped to shreds by a pack of lions.

"Chief forgive me for speaking out of turn, but Alex is finding it a challenge to inform you. There was an accident. The Jeep lost traction on the road on our way here and we collided with a tree. Your son, Jelani was seriously injured in the accident. We tried our best to sustain his injuries, but he developed a critical fever and fell into a coma. Considering the confined restraints of medical care, there was nothing we could do for him. It pains me to inform you that your son subsequently died from extensive injuries to his abdomen. He was a fearless man and a true warrior right until the end. I am truly sorry for your loss."

While Sam perfectly executed the bad news, Alex sat in silent awe. That did sound a lot better than the version she was hopelessly preparing in her mind. So effortless but yet with the utmost warmth and tenderness in his voice and eyes. Even though he didn't mention anything about the lions, he conveyed the exact sequence of the events that led up to Jelani's death. The chief's grim look said he didn't need to know the rest. How it happened wouldn't change that his son was dead. But it still didn't explain where his body was.

"I assume, as is customary, that you probably want a traditional river burial and we tried carrying him for a very long time but, ahem..." Alex cleared her throat again and Sam cut in.

"Circumstances prevented us from carrying him over such a huge distance. We took it upon ourselves and buried him under a tall, strong tree and gave him a small ceremony in his honor."

Sam came to her rescue again even though it wasn't entirely the truth. Somehow, though she didn't agree with lying, Alex knew the details wouldn't benefit anyone.

And with that the chief seemingly heard enough as his elders gathered around him in consult. If they didn't accept their story as the truth, they could be rejected from the tribe, or worst, put to death. It felt like eternity before the chief finally spoke.

"Thank you Lakicia, Mr. Quinn. We will hold a ceremony in my son's honor tonight as we celebrate his life and submit his spirit to the gods."

When the chief disappeared into his boma without speaking another word, Alex sat back angry and confused over the lack of emotion Jelani's father displayed.

"That's it? That's all he has to say after losing his only son? Why am I the only one who is angry here?"

"People deal with death differently, Alex. Some make it a public display, and others do it in solitude. In the end, death is no man's friend and he now has the task of delivering the news to Jelani's wife and child. I'm assuming that's who just followed him in?"

Alex covered her face with her hands and turned towards Sam, burying her head in the nook between his neck and shoulder. "Oh no, you're right, that's Jelani's wife and his little girl. I forgot all about them. Oh, this is unbearable."

"I am so sorry that it has come to this Alex. It is not easy losing someone you care for and far less even having to deliver the news to their loved ones. Tonight we will mourn with them and build up our strength. Tomorrow we need to face the new day and find your father."

Alex barely knew Sam, but the longer she spent time with him, the more she wanted to learn more about him. She quietly thanked Professor Keating for his apt selection. Sitting there with him made her feel safe. Like she didn't have to worry about making things work on her own anymore. She shared her burden, and he shared his strength. Something told her they would be friends for years to come.

The evening, much to her surprise, was a jubilant and festive affair. It was entirely the opposite of the small family memorial they had for her mother. Instead, the tribe prepared a feast fit for a king and dressed up in strikingly decorated tribal wear. It was colorful and cheery filled with music and dance as the entire village came together and celebrated Jelani's life rather than his death. All evening, not one single tear lay on anyone's cheek, not even his wife's.

"Have you ever seen a funeral this happy? I mean it's an amazing way to pay your last respects, isn't it?" Sam said.

"For sure, I mean if you think about it, we throw parties when babies are born so why shouldn't we throw a party when someone close to us goes off to a better place? It's just the sadness we don't deal with so well. The fact that you know, while you are partying away the night, they are not at the party with you nor would you ever see them again."

"Yeah but we are rather selfish then isn't it? We think of our sadness and loss first before we think of where they might be? Have you ever thought that they might be happier in heaven than on earth?" Sam asked.

His question silenced her tongue. She wasn't even sure how to answer him.

"Do you mean you believe there is a heaven?"

"Don't you?"

"Not sure, I have never really thought of it much. I mean, I guess your spirit has to go somewhere right?"

"So after your mother died, did you not sense or feel her with you at times?"

"Perhaps yes, sometimes. What I mean is that I don't know for sure if it was my mother or just my imagination."

"I am a man of science Alex, and let me tell you what I have learned over my years of being a physician having to watch people die before my eyes. I see some with tormented looks in their eyes just before they cross over, and then I know they have not found peace on earth to move over to the other side. Then there are others who literally die with a smile on their face. Those are the ones who go to heaven. And I would far rather go to heaven than to hell. So yes, I believe in heaven and in hell. If I don't, then what else is there to believe in?"

Faith was a troubling concept for Alex. She remembered how her mother told her the very same thing Sam just did some time back. 'Life is not worth living without faith,' she used to say. Perhaps this man, Sam Quinn, was sent from the very heaven they believe in, an angel in human embodiment. Someone to rescue her from herself.

Alex fiddled with the flower that one of the little ones placed in her hair when they first arrived. She pondered whether Sam was her soulmate and if he was the very one whose sentences she would finish. What if he was the one her mother always said she would meet someday and stay with for the rest of her life?

That last thought scared her. A lifetime with someone was something she was not prepared to do. But beyond putting up with their idiosyncrasies for life, he had to put up with an agoraphobic wife. No man would ever want that.

"We should get some sleep, Alex. We need our strength to find your father before..."

Sam didn't finish his sentence, but Alex knew all too well what he was about to say.

CHAPTER TEN

3 YEARS AGO - IZZY

"Are you sure you need to go Charles? We can hold off and wait for you to hurry back?"

Charles chuckled at Izzy's plea for him to stay.

"Look after your mum okay, Alexandra? She thinks she can't do this without me; as if she needs any of my help finding Rhapta. But let me tell you something, there is no stopping your mother. Once she is out there doing her thing she's like a bull in Pamplona. Just you wait and see."

"I still think you should pop over to London, finish the business as quick as you can and hurry back so we can make this discovery together," Izzy made a final effort to persuade Charles to stay.

He planted a kiss on her forehead.

"Izzy my love, it is time to spread your wings and do this on your own. It is your dream, remember? I'm going to take care of business back home so we can take this thing to the very end. Make us proud. You can do this."

He gave her one last kiss on the mouth before he drove off to the airport. His mind had been fixed and there was no changing it now.

"Have a safe flight Charles," Izzy added as she watched her husband drive away.

She wasn't quite sure why she was so emotional. It wasn't as if her husband had never gone off somewhere without her. But something that day was different from the times he left her behind before.

She stood watching the cloud of dust in the road long after he left. She just couldn't shake the feeling she had in the pit of her stomach. Like something terrible was about to happen. In the depths of her heart she didn't want Charles to leave her, not this time. A sudden rush of fear propelled an intense vulnerability and precariousness within her and for the first time in a long time, she silently sobbed.

"We will be fine Mum, really. Let him do what he needs to, and we will focus on finding Rhapta okay? You can do this," Alex consoled. "Besides we ought to get cracking to the river before the sun sits too high. Come. The chase waits for no one right?" Quoting one of Charles's favorite phrases.

"Now you sound just like your Dad you silly girl." Izzy let off a nervous giggle before they turned and made their way to their new dig site.

The river was fast flowing and opened its mouth into the turquoise ocean off the East coast of Tanzania.

"It's a paradise isn't it Mum? I mean look at these crystal clear waters."

"I can't agree more, my love. See that island there? Can you still remember which island that is? That's Zanzibar remember? And that one there, is Mafia Island. They call these the Spice Islands because they were one of the first islands trading spices between the Middle East and Africa. In fact, they still do. We believe Rhapta disappeared under the ocean right around here and it is in this riverbed your Dad and I found the first pieces of ancient pottery years ago. We should start our search somewhere in this vicinity."

Izzy turned to the crew behind her. They were patiently waiting for her instructions. Now this was precisely where Charles usually took over and whipped their camp in order before anyone could say, 'dig for gold.' Never once had she done any of their explorations without Charles by her side. She needed to stay focused and fake her way through it.

And miraculously she did manage to get into Charles's head, and within an hour and a half, their campsite was up and running like clockwork. And if she was honest, far quicker and more efficient than when her husband did it. When the crew finished and retired for the night, Alex and she settled in their own tent.

"See Mum. Dad was right. You are a natural with all this stuff. Now, if only we can figure out what this cipher was for, right? Do you think it is quite literally a key we have to find? And even if it were an actual key, where would it go? I don't see any buildings around here. Perhaps another wooden box or something?"

"It could be, although, I think it might in effect be more like a fundamental solution. Like it is the key to something that holds together important things, a clue that will unlock another riddle or part of the puzzle. The question is what though? I feel like we're missing something."

Izzy paced the small three by four tent and heard the sound of twigs breaking under feet outside. Alexandra heard it too. They froze and waited in an attempt to figure out what it was.

It was close to midnight, and the crew would have already been asleep so it was highly unlikely to be any of them. The thought of it being animals was more probable although lions and elephants rarely ventured so close to the beach. There was a definite chance of it being salt water crocodiles. With their camp sitting right on the river mouth it was rare, but certainly not impossible. But Izzy's instinct alarmed her to the fact that it could just as well be imposters. She silently wished Charles was with them, but consoled herself in the knowledge that she was a strong independent woman with a daughter to protect.

Keeping a gun was something Charles, and she started doing many years back when they had first encountered artifact traders. They were not as friendly as they had hoped, and Charles and she found themselves in a couple of sticky situations over the years. This was certainly not the first time they had uninvited guests around their camp. Charles and Izzy were unlike so many of the greedy treasure hunters looking for a quick fortune so when they were hot on the trail of a new relic, these fortune seekers would snoop around their camps for clues.

Izzy placed her index finger on her lips for Alex to be quiet and tip-toed over to her stretcher for her rifle that lay hidden inside her sleeping bag.

She could hear her heartbeat throb in her inner ear. It was eerily quiet apart from the gentle waves that flowed out onto the sandy beach. She signaled for Alexandra to turn the lamp down, and then slowly moved toward the door flap. Her stomach threatened to push into her throat, and a heat wave engulfed her. She struggled to steady her rifle in her sweaty palms. The noise was right outside their tent. It was undoubtedly footsteps. If it was a crocodile that was crawling around outside his tail would have been swooshing in the sand. She was sure the sound was human. Izzy peeped through the slight gap between the tent's walls. Her instincts were right. It was a human. She just couldn't quite make out who.

"Can you see any—"?

Izzy stopped her daughter from finishing her question and quietly mouthed, "There's a man outside."

"Who?" Alex mouthed back only to have her mother shrug her shoulders.

Izzy gripped the rifle handle and slowly pulled the tent flap aside with the barrel. The stranger wasn't behind the tent anymore, so she looked back at Alex who stood in silent fear. Alex who had been hiding in the back of the tent, suddenly jumped forward as another crackling noise sounded from outside the tent right behind her.

"Shh," Izzy gestured again before whispering, "Stay here."

"Mum no! Don't go out on your own," Alex whispered back in angst.

But Izzy knew they couldn't just ignore it. "I'll be fine, just stay where you are okay?"

The moon was full that night and it shone a bright torch-light over the calm waters and their campsite. Good or bad, she needed to investigate who or what was lurking behind their tent. The moonlight would help to find the intruder, but equally, he could see her.

Izzy sent up a quick prayer. Careful to not give her position away she tip-toed baby steps on the sand around the back of the tent. The moon's light cast a shadow of one single person in her direction. She gripped her gun and put her finger on the trigger, ready to shoot. Her heartbeat in her ears drummed out any chance of hearing anything else to the point that she had to strain her ears. She moved ever so slowly, step by step, until she had a better view.

A little bit further...a little more...almost...

"Eric? Eric is that you?" Finally spotting a man that looked vaguely like Eric.

"Hey-ey Izzy. The one and only yes."

Then he spotted her gun.

"Whoa! You won't shoot your trusted assistant now, would you?" Giving a sarcastic, sheepish giggle.

Izzy lowered the gun in line with her waist, not totally at ease with his sarcastic mocking.

"What the heck are you doing outside my tent in the middle of the night, Eric? And where on earth have you been? You disappeared for days without a word to anyone."

Eric's nervous display on his face didn't go unnoticed. She sensed he was hiding something. That sheepish smile looked like she might have just caught him with his hand in the cookie jar.

"Speak up Eric. What are you doing here and where have you been?"

"Nowhere, I've been around site."

"You're lying. We looked everywhere for you before we left."

"How did you even find us? We left the last dig site undecided where we were going to settle so how did you know where we'd be?"

"Sorry for scaring you, Izzy, I'm glad I finally found you though. I had some urgent family business to attend to so I went into town to deal with a couple of things."

"Is that so? Urgent family business is it?"

She didn't trust this boy as far as she could throw him. Her father always warned her against redheads when she was a child.

"Indeed yes, like I said, family business. When I got back to the site, the villagers said you had gone."

"And? How exactly did you find us?"

Eric struggled to find the words,

"You heard me, Eric. How did you find us? And the camera? Why did you take the camera with you?"

"I guess Lady Luck was on my side. I have a nose for these things, you know."

"Mum, is everything all right?" Alex popped out from inside the tent.

"Everything's fine Alexandra. Eric decided to finally show up again. Go back inside," Izzy said sternly.

"Oh hello Eric. Where have you been? We needed the photos and now Dad—"

"Alexandra, please go back inside."

Izzy's instincts were on high alert. Something in the pit of her stomach didn't quite sit right. Eric's face was an open book and she could tell he was up to no good. She scoured the trees behind him to see if he was alone. It was hard to see beyond the dark shadows between the trees.

"I'm waiting, Eric, talk. Where is the camera and how did you find us?" Izzy pushed again.

"Well, Izzy. Your question is somewhat of a tricky one to answer. I went into town to buy new batteries for my camera and well the two shop owners bamboozled me. The crooks managed to swap my camera with theirs right in front of my very eyes, I tell you. I ended up at the police station, and they kept the camera as part of their evidence."

"WHAT? Please tell me you took the memory stick out?"

"Yes, of course, right here, see?" Handing the small black rectangle to Izzy.

"Well, I suggest you knock on the crew's tents and bunk with one of them tonight. We'll pick this up again in the morning. There's a lot of work to do tomorrow."

"Aye-Aye Ma'm, your wish is my command," Eric responded, his voice laden with sarcasm and Izzy watched as he rushed off to one of the crew's tents before heading back into her own tent.

Eric's story reeked of lies. She smelled trouble and was positive something was amiss. Her rifle was not going to leave her side that night.

"Mum, are you okay? What's going on?"

"I'm fine sweetheart. Eric has come back all of a sudden with some tall story of having had family trouble or something."

"But that's good isn't it? I mean we were looking for him so now he can help, right?"

She had always been such a naive girl; always believing the best about people.

"Oh, you're so naive, Alexandra. It is great that you always believe the best about people, but always watch your back, my darling. Things aren't always as they seem. I'll sort it out in the morning. For now, we need to get some sleep. We have a lost city to find tomorrow."

Izzy gave her a quick hug and turned in for the night. But her head whirled with suspicion over Eric's disappearance and sudden return. Something about his story troubled her and kept her up most of the night.

They started bright and early the next day. Enthusiasm buzzed among the crew as they ardently worked the dig site. They were trusted colleagues that have been at it almost for as long as Charles and Izzy had. They were just as excited to finally find the infamous lost city of Rhapta. Most of them were native Tanzanians so for them it wasn't the treasure that spurred them on. They sought reverence from their tribe for being part of history in discovering something most thought never existed. Their pride was everything to them and yet they were the most humble people on earth.

The elders held firm in their belief that Rhapta was a burial ground for their ancestors and that the land and its people would be cursed if they disturbed it so they insisted on being part of the process and prevent the curse of Kifa.

Bottle caps and scrap metal periodically triggered the metal detectors that, after a while, evoked little surprise. Izzy kept her eye on Eric, scrutinizing his every move. He was his old silent self again, without exception hovering around the site with his journal and auxiliary camera. Like a vulture flying overhead waiting for his prey to die before moving in.

Alexandra took her dad's place and was right beside her mother, sifting and brushing the dig.

Well into their week, with no new relics or any further evidence to speak of, the two crew members Izzy commissioned to dig further down the coast came running toward her, hands waving in the air with excitement.

"Izzy! Come look! We found strange rock formations that bare striking similarities to possible ruins. We found about five of them sticking out the water! Hurry! Once the high tide pushes in, they will disappear under the surface."

The news washed a wave of relief over the diligent crew that tediously worked with no results whatsoever since they got here. So Alex and Izzy scooped up their equipment and hurriedly followed the men to the discovery site. Eric, of course, was steadily in tow.

They walked about a mile down the coast when they spotted the square rock formations sticking up from the water.

They were right. The tide would completely cover the rock formations and without question hide them from anyone, even a trained eye.

"What do you think Mum? They certainly bear similarities to ruins. Do you think we finally found Rhapta?"

Izzy giggled. Not sure if it stemmed from excitement or total disbelief. Perhaps it was a little bit of both.

"All I can say, Alexandra, is that from this angle, I will eat my hat if it isn't an ancient ruin."

She turned her attention to Eric. "Take a couple of pics and make sure you send them across to Charles immediately. We need his input on this one."

She stood back as he photographed several pictures not taking her eyes off him once.

"Make sure you get some close-ups, and don't disappear anywhere again."

"Yes Ma'am."

The surface of the large grey boulders was flawless and riveting. Unlike the typical ragged rocks with sharp edges, these were perfectly smooth and shaped into identical rectangles with pristinely cut corners.

"How in heaven's name did they get it so precise and even? It's remarkable isn't it Mum?"

"Indeed sweetheart, quite a piece of engineering considering they had no laser cutting technology or anything of the likes back then."

Alex noticed something as she stood over one of them.

"Mum look. It seems there are bubbles coming up from underneath here. Perhaps a cave?"

Izzy peered into the water. "Alexandra, you're right. I spot oxygenation on these edges here, and the water seems clearer here too. We'll have to send some divers down to know for sure but it might very well be from an underwater cave. Check on the timetable for us please and get the crew to mark the coordinates. We need to get a dive in during high tide. Low tide diving could be fatal."

"Sure thing, but I am definitely calling Dad first. These formations are far too impressive to leave for later. He has to see this." Alex yanked her laptop from her backpack. It took a couple of attempts at connecting the internet having to move continually from spot to spot for a signal but it wasn't long before they heard Charles's voice over the laptop. Izzy marveled at the ease of technology and recalled having to rely on sending telegrams if they wanted to convey urgent news when she was a child.

"Dad! Guess what? We found it! I think we found it. Look!" Alex's voice echoed into her laptop where she tilted the screen up and turned it so Charles could see the ruins.

"It looks like ancient ruins, all right. Did you take some samples yet? Check for sulfur okay? Sometimes there are underground caves with sulfur so be careful," Charles replied.

"I think we spotted a possible cave earlier yes. We are sending some divers down at high tide. Mum sent for the team at the Aquatic some time ago. When are you coming back? Eric is back. He said he needed to take care of some family issues in town. That's why he was missing."

"Well, that's good Alexandra. Tell him to send the photos across urgently so I can study them. We might be on the cusp of the discovery of the century."

Izzy looked across at where Eric was a mere five minutes earlier. Once again, he was missing. When she called out for him, he didn't answer either.

"Stupid boy is MIA again," she spat.

"What's your mother complaining about?" Charles laughed from the other side of the line.

Izzy moved over to where Alex was sitting down on one of the formations still chatting to her father.

"Hello, my love. Nothing wrong with your ears is there? Eric is MIA, again. We found him spying outside our tent past midnight last night. I have no idea how he found us either, but that boy I'm telling you is up to no good."

"Calm down Izzy dear. I'm sure he has gone back to camp to process the photographs or something. Wrap up the samples and keep me posted okay?"

"Sure thing Charles. How are things going there?"

"Oh, same old same old Izzy. You know how it goes with these benefits. Boring as anything. But it looks like we are making headway, mind you, we will only really know once those donations come in."

. . .

A s Izzy and the crew wrapped for the day she silently cast a warning for Eric to be at the campsite when they arrived. She vowed that if he wasn't back at camp sending the photos to Charles, she would wring his neck herself for pulling another disappearing act.

But , as luck would have it, he sat behind his computer downloading the photos, leaving her somewhat disappointed in the wake of the certainty that he wouldn't be at camp. Still suspicious she glanced over his shoulder to see what he was up to and caught a glimpse of an email before he quickly changed the screen to a blown-up photo of the newly found ruins. Izzy felt that inkling sense in the pit of her stomach again. Her gut had never let her down yet. She knew he was up to something.

"Who's that email going to Eric?"

She caught him by surprise and watched as he fumbled for words, turning bright red in the process.

"Oh, uh just family business. Won't happen on the clock again Izzy."

'Family business' my foot, Izzy thought.

CHAPTER ELEVEN

ALEX

"Good morning Quinn. You look almost as good as the day on the plane." Alex giggled when Sam met up with her in the center of the village the next morning. They both managed to get a decent night's rest and a fresh change of clothes; albeit borrowed from one of the villagers.

"Not too bad yourself Miss Hunt."

Sam skimmed her loaned attire that seemed like she stepped back into the eighties and his eyes lingered a tad too long for her liking.

"Ahem," she cleared her throat and folded her arms in an awkward attempt to hide her discomfort; forcing his attention back to her face.

"How's your head?" Sam smiled at her embarrassment.

"Not too bad, thanks. And your hands?" The small talk continued.

"Remarkably, my hands are almost back to normal. It seems these native herbs they dressed it with did the job. Pretty impressive."

"It's the aloe. Out here it grows everywhere. The locals squeeze out the sap and grind the stems into a pulp. It's supposed to remove all infections and inflammation."

"Well, it sure as heck did that and some. Another couple of days and we will probably be able to take your stitches out. Did you sleep okay?"

Alex wasn't sure where their idle chitchat was going. She wasn't comfortable around men under normal circumstances, so this was too close for comfort.

"We don't have time for small talk Quinn. We need to find my father."

And with that snippy comment Alex spun around and headed off towards the chief's hut.

"Chief? Can we talk, please? We need to find my father. Can you help us, please?"

She took out her map and spread it open in front of him.

"Do you have any idea where they might have taken him?"

"I'm not sure Lakicia. Jelani—" He paused and rid the lump in his throat with a small cough. He was still trying to come to terms with the death of his son and needed to remind himself that he was not there any longer.

"Jelani said he thought it could have been the River Rebels. They are in this territory over here," pointing to a spot on the map.

"I will send a search party again to see if they can find out anything more."

"But there is a chance he might have escaped Chief so if this is in fact their location he could be anywhere on foot between here and here," circling and marking the areas off on her map.

She started pacing the chief's hut, snapping a twig between her fingers. She needed to think like her father. Get into his head and figure out where he might have taken up hiding if he managed to escape them. Where was the one place he would hide?

Then it came to her. "The safe house! He could have made it to the safe house! If he escaped, which he might have, then he would have headed directly there. Okay, it is quite a distance to walk but my Dad's tough. He would have found a way, I'm certain. Chief, could you assemble some men to check up the river toward the River Rebels' territory, please? Sam and I will head off to the safe house. I'm sure he's there. He has to be."

Alex crammed the map back into her backpack and excitedly turned to face Sam.

"Let's go, Quinn. We don't have any time to spare."

"And how are you planning on getting wherever there is, Alex?" Sam replied looking puzzled.

"You're welcome to take any of the canoes or the *piki-piki*."

The Chief pointed to an antiquated motorcycle under a flysheet next to his boma. With what was their only Jeep destroyed in the accident, other than a bicycle or the boat the *piki-piki* might be the faster option by far.

"That way you two lovebirds can sit closely together," the chief added with a sheepish smile.

"Lovebirds! No, you got it all wrong, Chief. We are not lovebirds or anything of the sort. Sam is just an assistant assigned by the university to help me. We have a mission and that's it."

"Lakicia. I might be an old man, but I am not the chief for nothing. My wise eyes have already seen. He looks to be a good man."

"Oh, don't be childish Chief. I don't have time for silly business. I need to find my father."

He chuckled as Alex turned and hurried out of the hut, grateful that Sam couldn't understand a word of their Swahili conversation. If only she could be certain he didn't see her blush for he'd definitely put two and two together.

T he dirt road from the village into Dar es Salaam was a bumpy and torturously slow one. The heavy torrential storms from the night before dug massive potholes and puddles of muddy water everywhere. Debris of broken branches lay scattered across the road, making it harder to navigate around.

"If you grip me any tighter Alex, I might have to stop the motorcycle."

Alex ignored Sam's flirtatious comment although the prospect of his intention sent a flurry of emotions through her insides.

"You're driving like a maniac, Quinn. How else am I supposed to stay on?"

Or did he? Could the Chief be right? Was there something brewing between them without her even realizing it? She liked him more than she thought possible. He was extremely caring and he shared the same adventurous spirit. She couldn't deny that there was something magical happening between them. But the thought scared her more than it enticed her. Her life was not one to be shared with anyone. Once she was back home and everything was over, she'd retreat into her apartment and carry on with her research. That was all she wanted. It was best that way.

And for the immediate moment, there was too much on her plate to waste time on such nonsense.

"How much further?" She yelled across to the armed guide on the *piki-piki* in front of them. The chief didn't want to risk anything and insisted one of his men accompanied them, guns and all.

"Not far, almost there Miss Lakicia."

"Why do they keep calling you Lakicia?" Sam asked.

"It's a name Jelani gave me when I was little."

"What does it mean?"

"It means she who is favored among people."

"Were you?"

"Was I what?"

"Everyone's favorite?"

"Watch where you're going, Quinn. You're going to get us both killed before we even hit the city."

She chose not to answer him. If she let him into her world even further, she might never get him out, and as it stood, he already cracked her shell more than she had wanted. No, this venture was nothing but a rescue mission, nothing more.

Saved by the guide's announcement that they had reached the outskirts of the city, Alex spotted some outlying buildings up ahead and they pulled over to the side of the road.

"Here I stop. You go alone," the guide informed them and handed each of them a gun before driving back to the village.

Alex had never held a gun before much less had ever needed to use one but, under the circumstances, she agreed it was necessary. Her parents had one but they never had need for it either.

"It isn't an egg Alex. Here, let me show you. Hold it like this. Always pointing to the ground and away from people. See this? This pin is the safety. Now it's on, and now it's off. Keep it on for now, the safety that is, okay? We don't want you to fire at anything accidentally."

"Where did you learn all this?" Surprised by how comfortable Sam was with a weapon.

"Let's just say my old man is a bit of a gun enthusiast. He took me shooting clay pigeons when I was little. We used to visit the local shooting range quite often. It was his way of preparing for the world coming to an end so he needed to make sure we could defend ourselves."

Alex bit her bottom lip. She didn't like guns or violence. It made her nervous and meant trouble.

"Alex, you'll be fine. I got you, remember? It might be a good idea if we shot one or two practice rounds; so you can get the feel of it, yes?"

"Oh no, I don't think that is such a great idea. No-no, we are never going to need it anyway. Let's just go."

Alex wiped the tear that threatened to run down her face as she recalled the last time she had to handle a gun.

"Everything will be fine Alex. I promise you. We are going to find your father and all go home safely. Trust me. We'll do this together every step of the way."

"I'm scared, Quinn. What if my father is dead?"

"Alex, look at me. He's not, okay? I've studied your parents from the moment I learned to read. I know just about everything there is to know about them. Your father is one of the toughest guys there is with a lot of knowledge and street smarts. He knows how to get himself out of tight spots. Like when they were in China, and the government threatened to cease their dig. He wouldn't have made National Geographic if he wasn't something to write about, Alex. If you don't want to use the gun, then that's okay too. We'll take it easy. Deal?"

He did it again, calmed her down and kept her from losing control of the situation. She had no idea how he managed to do it or even why she always felt safe around him. She believed every word he said.

"Put your gun here, in the back of your pants under your shirt, like this."

His hand on the small of her back gave her more assurance that Sam Quinn had her back; literally and figuratively. And she liked it that way. But her head still ruled her heart and defenses built around it.

"Thanks, I got it, Quinn. Now, let's go. I'll drive."

"You're the boss," taunting her with a sideways smile.

The familiar road to the safe house was one her father made a point of them memorizing; even at night. As a child, she never quite figured out why he insisted they remember the way. He made her mother and her walk there from all the different routes into the city. But as Alex and Sam approached the location, she understood why. She was too young to grasp it back then but it was now obvious her parents were faced with dangerous situations then already. There was no question about it. Rhapta caused much controversy in Tanzania over the years, and when treasure-hunting fever lured them from all over the world, it created greed and envy that pushed the hobby to a new level. They needed to be alert and ready for anything.

"Keep your eyes open for anyone following us Quinn."

"Aye-aye, Captain."

He was playfully mocking her to keep the situation light, as usual. She regretted snapping at him earlier. Her aloof behavior was the only thing that kept her emotions—and people—at bay.

She kept her eye on the side view mirror. There was no indication of anything out of the ordinary behind them. To be safe, she crisscrossed the streets intentionally throwing anyone off their trail. Just in case. She couldn't take any chances. If her father did escape the rebels and was at the safe house as she suspected, the rebels would have eyes all over the city.

Dar es Salaam was bustling with African traders and tourists making it ever more challenging to maneuver the bike amongst them. They made their way to the safe house slowly.

As Alex turned the corner her eye caught sight of a military green four-wheeler in her side mirror. It wasn't the first time she had spotted it. She was certain it was the same one she saw behind them a little earlier. There was only one way to find out, so she took the first alleyway left and then turned right into another; all the while keeping her eye on the mirror. And sure enough, there they were. She needed no more convincing. They were indeed following them, and they were slowly but surely gaining on them. It was nearly impossible to see who was inside the vehicle but she wasn't about to find out either.

"Hold on Quinn. Don't look now but we're being followed."

"What exactly do you mean when you say, 'hold on' ?"

But before she could explain, she accelerated and she felt Sam tighten his grip around her waist. She kicked the bike into lower gear and opened the throttle. It wasn't the fastest bike on the planet, but the fact that it was smaller and fit through the side alleys played to their advantage. The Jeep wasn't far behind. She had to find a way to shake them off their tail. Her mind jumped ahead as she mapped the roads. She knew the city streets like the back of her hand. Deciding the market square would be their best recourse she took the next corner, almost throwing Sam off again. It was midday and the square would be packed with tourists shopping at the local vendors. She could easily cut through with the bike; their followers, not so much.

"Take it easy! Where did you learn to ride like this?" Sam yelled from behind her.

But Alex was focused and determined. She did not bat an eye and kept taking sharp turns left and then right to throw the Jeep off their tail.

The square was up ahead, and it was indeed teeming with people. It would be tough for the stalkers to keep up with them now. If she managed to cut through the crowds and crossed the square they'd be fine.

"Can you see them, Quinn?"

"If you're talking about the green SUV then no. We lost them when you first turned into the square and almost threw me off."

"Great! That means they have to drive all the way around the square to get to the other side and that could take forever in this traffic. There's no way they'd track us once I get over the bridge."

"How far to the safe house?"

"Not far, it's straight ahead."

Ten minutes later Alex and Sam reached the safe house. Deciding she needed to make certain the Jeep hadn't caught up with them, she took a slow drive around the block. Her eyes remained peeled for imminent threats. She was relieved when her safety check revealed there were none.

The abandoned warehouse looked exactly as she remembered it. From the outside, everything appeared to be intact apart from a few broken windows at the top. She was taught not to park directly in front of the entrance. Her father was always very specific about it being another last safety protocol. So she parked the bike around the back behind a nearby building. They had to go at it on foot and quickly. It wouldn't be wise to linger and risk being seen.

"Come on Quinn. Keep up. We have to get inside before they track us down."

At the front door, Alex paused and surveyed the street once more.

"I think we've lost them Alex. I don't see anyone. Not that I'm surprised after your daredevil driving," Sam joked as he smoothed his hand up and down the wooden door.

"Is this the front door? Where's the door knob? How the heck do we get inside the building?"

"Yes, it's the door. Move over."

The lack of a door handle was a decoy. Instead, a brass rhinoceros head decorated the door, camouflaged as a door knocker. She pushed its right eye and waited for the clicking sound. Next, she twisted the horn to the left to hear another click, before she then pulled the right ear that led to another click and a second later, the large wooden door released.

"What the...? Well, what do you know? That's cracking. A secret lock. I would have never guessed it," Sam exclaimed in amazement.

Alex rushed inside. "Dad! Daddy? Are you here? It's me, Alexandra."

Her words echoed in the hollowness of the warehouse, and she paused briefly to listen for her father's answer. But he didn't answer. It was quiet. Satisfied he wasn't downstairs, she rushed down the corridor and leaped up the staircase to the room on the loft level. There was a chance he'd be there considering it was the bedroom. But as they reached the top of the stairs, they heard a rustling noise come from somewhere downstairs.

"Someone is definitely here Quinn," she whispered. She yanked him by his arm to follow her back down the stairs and into the cavity below the stairs. If there was someone downstairs and her father was up in the bedroom, she'd expose him.

"Now would be a good time to take your gun out and take it off safety Alex."

"Not a chance, you do it. As long as you don't get trigger-happy and shoot at anything that moves. It might be my father so be careful."

"Have you forgotten I'm a doctor? I took the Hippocratic oath. I'll shoot to incapacitate only. And then I'll probably run over and fix him up."

"Shh, now's not the time for jokes, Quinn. We could actually be killed here today."

"Okay, okay, just saying."

"There's only one way into the upstairs room. If we can get in we would have eyes on every corner in this building. If my father was up there, he would have certainly seen us by now already. I think someone else is here."

"Who else knows of this place?"

"No one, just my father and I. And my mother knew of course, but she's, well, you know." Alex trailed off unable to still speak the words out loud.

"I don't see anyone, Alex. It could just as well have been a rat or the pigeons or something. Let's take a chance and head up the stairs."

Alex agreed and allowed Sam to lead the way up the stairs. She might have looked calm and in control on the outside, but her pounding heart in her ears said the opposite. Her palms were clammy and that familiar feeling of fear gripped at the back of her neck. She was desperate for her pills. The memory of how she lost them in the first place, didn't help her anxiety in that moment either. She was ready to pass out, but she couldn't allow herself to be weak, not now. Her father needed her and she had to do whatever it took to save him.

Once at the top of the stairs, Alex took a deep breath and pressed her thumb on the small screen that was hidden below the railing. A latch above her head flew open where she pushed a small button to release the door.

"What is this place? It's amazing," Sam whispered in awe behind her. "It's like being inside Pharaoh's tomb or something. You're one heck of a family that's for sure."

With the door firmly closed behind them, Alex walked over to the only window in the room. She peaked outside behind the curtain to survey the street. There was no sign of anyone outside. The bathroom looked like it had been used and there was fresh food in the fridge. There were clearly signs that indicated someone had been living there. Over at the bed she pulled the top cover away to reveal fresh, clean linen. The wardrobe had a few items of men's pants and shirts but it could have just as well belonged to her father. She pulled out one of the books in the bookshelf and a door to a small room popped open. Inside the monitor for the surveillance cameras was off. She hastily switched it on and flicked from one camera view to another. She knew that the noise came from somewhere but the cameras covered every inch of the warehouse and there was no one there.

"Well, I hate to break it to you, but it very much looks like someone is staying here and whoever it is, has a map and several notes on Rhapta."

"What?" Alex rushed over to where Sam sat behind the desk skimming through the umpteen notes and scribbles.

"These are my mother's notes. It's her handwriting. Someone stole all her research. What the...! Who the heck would do such a despicable thing? And how? How would they have found them?"

"She must have had them on her when they took her, or they came back for it afterward."

"No, I don't think so. She didn't have it on her and we were practically asleep when...when, it's not possible. Her bag with her journal was on the floor next to her bed, and they never came inside the tent that night."

"Well, someone is living in this place. It's not the cleanest, but you can most definitely see someone is living here. Look. There is half a sandwich here, and it looks only about a day or two old."

Perplexed Alex flicked through the camera views again to see if she might have missed anyone downstairs.

"See anything?"

"Nope, nothing. I'm not convinced that noise was a rat or a pigeon, Sam. I'm telling you. We're not alone in here.

"I thought you said only you, and your parents had knowledge of the safe house"

"Yes, and my Dad's clearly not here and my Mum's dead so that leaves an intruder. We have no choice but to wait it out and surprise him. Sooner or later he would have to come upstairs. We'll be here waiting for him."

CHAPTER TWELVE

CHARLES

The stabbing pain in his feet restricted his running. It didn't help that the boots were about two sizes too big either.

"Darn shoes of a dead man," he scoffed out loud.

Charles was angry. It wasn't supposed to go down like this. He loved his job and over the years had more than his fair share of hair-raising expeditions, but this? This one set the bar. It was a question of life and death; death in Izzy's case. His mind wandered with every step Charles took as it produced all the questions that had been torturing him for years. Was all this worth losing her life over? A ridiculous quest for a lost city that might never have existed in the first place. But his wife believed with all her heart that it was real and in his heart, he believed it too.

If only he hadn't left her and Alexandra alone. For years he tried to make sense of why they took Izzy. Her kidnappers must have known another piece of the puzzle and needed her to solve it. Everyone was well aware she was the brain behind the ciphers.

Charles stopped and leaned against a tree. He had to stop torturing himself. It wouldn't bring her back. Nothing would. But finding Rhapta and completing her dream would bring closure and set her soul free forever.

It was dark amongst the dense trees as the leaves blocked the moonlight. He had no idea of direction and could have been running in circles for all he knew. The tall grass and bushes were thick and not easy to navigate. Aside from that, he smelled of blood, which, out there in the African jungle, meant he was any carnivore's easy prey. He had to move quickly and quietly and get to safety. His feet hurt and he could barely see through his swollen eyes, but he was alive and that was all that counted.

Charles was exhausted but he kept running. Every couple of yards he made a small carving into a tree to mark his route. That way he'd know if he was running in circles. He managed to run a fair distance into the bush and was pretty sure no one was following him. He heaved heavily. His lungs were taking strain. A sharp burning sensation in his lungs caused him to gasp for breath. He wasn't as fit as he used to be.

The thought crossed his mind whether the rebels were aware of his escape or if they assumed the rivals took him as their prisoner. With any luck, they were all dead. Shot by the same sniper that killed the giant. His body ached in places he never knew was possible. Moving, much less running, was harder to do with each step he took. He had no idea how far he had run or how far he still had to go. He stumbled a few times. Partly due to the clumsy shoes and partly because he couldn't see much. But Charles kept running and never stopped or looked back.

He couldn't safely assume they weren't on the hunt for him. They needed the key. A key that didn't even exist. All he had knowledge of was the cipher code, nothing more. And now, because of his fabricated confession of Izzy being alive with a key, they would hunt him down until the end of time. Even more-so now than ever before. He regretted calling Alex when they were under attack. He wasn't thinking clearly and now he might have put her in harms way too.

He stopped for a brief moment to catch his breath and leaned against a tree trunk. His body ached all over. As he panted in a desperate attempt to get air into his strained lungs, he heard a loud hissing sound in front of him. It was quite dark under the tree, but the moonlight broke through the trees about half a yard in front of him. It was a cobra! His head was pulled back revealing his broad, flat hood and yellowish underbelly, almost glowing in the faint moonlight. His fangs were the size of a crocodile's teeth.

There was no mistaking the breed. It was an Egyptian Cobra; massive one too.

Charles might have stopped breathing altogether in that instant. Unable to breathe or move a muscle, he stared into the glowing eyes of the snake. cobras were known to move as fast as lightning, and he'd be dead in thirty minutes if he got bitten. From the corner of his eye, Charles caught the sudden movement of a rat close by. Much in the same way he did, the rat stopped dead in its tracks as he came face to face with the predator. Somewhat relieved, the rat was Charles' perfect distraction and it became evident the snake was now weighing up his options, swinging from side to side between rat and human. Charles transferred his thoughts onto the snake to choose the rat instead and when the rat thought he could outrun the snake, the cobra struck.

Occupied with his large catch Charles slowly stepped aside and once out of reach, started running as fast as his two lacerated feet could manage. When he was far enough away, he tried gaining his bearings and stopped for another brief second making sure not to lean against any trees again. The moonlight was stronger as it burst through the trees. It was safe to say he was out of the woods, so to speak. He needed to think logically. The rebel camp couldn't have been too far away from water. They captured him in the late afternoon and he had full sun on him while he was in their vehicle. That meant he faced west and they might have traveled north up the river.

So then it was likely he was somewhere north of Dar es Salaam and the village was south. He might be way off and sorely lacking any sense but it was his only shot.

He looked up at the stars between the tall trees. He'd have to get to a clearing with a better view of the constellations. On a clear night he could find better direction and find his way out of there. Happy with his conclusion, he started running again. He wasn't sure how long he could keep the pace. His body was close to collapse but he kept going.

What seemed like hours later, he finally got to a large clearing of grassland. In the full moon he saw it was yellow and dry not green and lush which meant he most probably ran too far off course. Despondent he heard lions in the distance. He wasn't the only creature seeking out clearings. Lions and rhinos liked them also. Charles walked out into the clearing with caution and looked up at the stars.

They were incredibly bright and clear, and he recalled the last night Izzy, and he spent together under the stars before he left for London the next day. She didn't want him to go. Perhaps if he had listened to her she would still be alive, and Alexandra wouldn't have fallen ill. His heart was heavy, gripped with deep sorrow for his wife and daughter. He would never see his wife again and there was a distinct possibility he'd never see his daughter either.

A single tear rolled down his cheek as he searched the stars for answers. Orion's bent hourglass torso shone brightly in the sky. And then he found it, Mintaka. The rightmost star in Orion's belt that set within a degree measure true east or west. He stacked his fists hand-over-hand from the horizon until he reached Mintaka. He carefully calculated the degrees of angle measure. A flicker of hope filled his heart as he established his direction. At peace with his conclusions, he set off at a more relaxed pace in an attempt to give his aching feet and body a slight bit of relief.

Somewhere deep into the night the conditions of his escape pushed his badly dehydrated and exhausted body beyond his limit of endurance. All the while, Charles kept his eyes peeled for wild animals and his focus on taking one step at a time. He needed to stay alert and not stop. There was no point in giving up now. He'd come too far. He had a daughter to think of now. As long as he had breath in his lungs he was determined to not have her lose another parent.

His thoughts were all that kept him going. Along the way he spotted several rhino under a tree. It piqued his interest, as he knew full well that animals only hid under trees if they expected bad weather. Charles looked up at the heavens. There was not a cloud in the sky, but there they were, huddled together under the tree. Their horns looked like beacons in the moonlight. Charles stopped to admire them and thought it sad that poachers felt the need to slaughter them just to sell their horns on the black market. He also knew that he needed to keep clear of them. They looked peaceful, but turned on you quickly if threatened.

The grass grew dense in some places where Charles had trouble walking through them. It most certainly proved he was close to water. He needed to rest and wondered if he still knew how to climb a tree. The image of the cobra entered his thoughts. The Savannah was prime habitat for all sorts of poisonous snakes and there was a firm chance he'd encounter some of the tree climbing ones. With not many options of where to rest, he decided to continue a little further. He should be close. He had been walking for hours on end.

A sudden lightning bolt flashed above his head illuminating the entire horizon. Moments later another bolt flashed and then another and another. A number of loud thunderous rumblings in between more lightning bolts confirmed that the rhino was on the mark after all. It wasn't long before Charles felt raindrops wet his face and out of nowhere, the heavens opened up and dumped bucket loads of refreshing rain over him.

"Hahaaaaa! Yes! Open your floodgates!" He shouted out loud, as he tried to find shelter.

Dehydrated and exhausted, he stuck out his tongue, desperate for some water to moisten his parched throat. The rain soothed his drought-stricken body and stung his still swollen and bruised face but he didn't complain. It was sheer bliss. He was conscious of the fact that he should run for cover from the lightning, but he just couldn't help it. His body was overriding his logic, hands-down. He needed water and fell to his knees. With outstretched arms he threw his head back and opened his mouth as wide as he could. The rain was like a river of pure gold flowing over him and down his arid throat. He never knew rainwater could taste that good. It was medicine to his defeated body—and mind.

The last time he danced in the rain like that was when Izzy and he first started dating. They managed to get a booking in that fancy French restaurant in Covent Garden. He had saved all his money just for that dinner with her. They hit a downpour just as they stepped out onto the sidewalk. Izzy wasn't like the other girls who squealed at the slightest drop of rain ruining their hairdos and fancy clothing. Instead, she opened her arms much like his were now and danced pirouettes around him. They were soaked, but it was one of the happiest times of his life. That's when he knew he needed to spend the rest of his life with her. And now, he stood there exposed in the rain barely alive and she was dead.

"Is this you Izzy my love? Is this you opening up the heavens and helping me through?" He shouted to the heavens.

He couldn't help but wonder if she was behind all that beautiful rain, reminding him of the good times they had. What he wouldn't do to dance in the rain with her again.

. . .

W hen the rain soaked his body enough for him to come to his senses, Charles decided to risk the storm and keep walking toward the dense trees in the distance. The night was a cold and certainly wet one, but at least the rain contained the predators and quenched his body.

It had been almost twelve days since he had been captured and tortured. At least that's the number he came up with. He had lost count. But his body was not as strong as his mind and when his knees caved and he fell with his face into the muddy grassland, he stayed down.

H e had no idea how long he lay face down in the rain, but when he finally managed to lift his head off the ground, the rain had stopped and the sun popped its head up just beyond the horizon. He lived to see another day and now the sun's rays were proof that he was heading east. His cracked lips burst open when he smiled. Izzy would have been so proud that he used the stars to navigate his course.

'Mark my words, Charles Benjamin Hunt. One day is one day you'll need those stars to show you the way' she once said to him when he argued the purpose of learning the constellations. And as always, she was right.

Somewhere between the hallucinations and dreams, Charles slipped off into a deep sleep. It was the incessant prodding of a stick and children's laughter that eventually woke him. It was hot and the sun's piercing rays forced him to shut his eyes again. He sat up and shielded his eyes. It wasn't a dream or a hallucination. Kids laughing and dancing surrounded him. They offered him water and tried to help him up.

"Take me to your village. Please, take me to your village!" He repeated in broken Swahili. It was only when he mentioned the chief's name that they stopped dancing.

"Your village, chief, help," he tried again.

One brave boy, about school going age, pulled him by his hand as the others pushed him from behind. In unison they pulled him across the sweltering Savannah and even when his feet shot stabbing pains up his legs, Charles was overjoyed. He had made it through the predator infested African Savannah and survived against all the odds. And up ahead the cheery cries of his village welcomed him home.

"Charlie-boy! We think you dead. You okay! You safe Charlie-boy? We so happy," the chief yelled as his tribe carried Charles in and lay him down on a cot.

"Charlie-boy, I'm so happy you're safe."

"Hello, Chief. I never thought I'd be this happy to see you."

"Where you been Charlie-boy?"

"The darn River Rebels were behind it. They think I have the key. Or more accurately, Izzy has the key."

"Izzy? What you mean old friend. Izzy with gods."

"Of course yes. She's not with us."

"So why you talk crazy? Izzy got the key. What you mean?"

"It was a little white lie that's all, nothing more. I needed to buy myself some time so I lied to the rebels and told them Izzy was still alive and that she had the key. If they thought she was alive and has the key then they would need me to get it. I bargained my life in exchange for a key that doesn't exist. They were going to kill me, and it was all I could think of telling them at the time."

"So they make you go?"

"No-no, not a chance, they'll be after me more now than ever. A group of rivals attacked them. I think they fought over territorial rights, so I managed to escape."

"You like James Bond Charlie-boy," packing a laugh.

"Are the crew and Jelani okay?" Charles asked.

The chief looked at his feet and shook his head.

"Jelani with gods. He no make it Charlie-boy."

"What? Jelani is...Jelani is dead? Those brutes! I'll get them for this."

"No Charlie-boy, not River Rebels. He die in car crash with Alex."

Charles thought he had heard wrong. Either that or he was hallucinating again. He smacked his cheek and shook his head vigorously before speaking again.

"Say what now chief? I don't think I heard you right. Alex? She's... she died with him?"

"NO Charlie-boy, she not die. She with Jelani in car. Jelani he dead. Alex, she alive."

Even the Chief's second explanation couldn't clear his confusion.

"Wait, Chief. My Alex is here? In the village?"

"Yes, Charlie-boy. She come with *Daktari*, they special friends."

"Doctor? Dr. Jones? Why did she come with Dr. Jones?"

"No no, not Jones, Quinn. Daktari Sam Quinn. She come with Quinn."

Charles scratched his head. "Who on earth is Sam Quinn? Special friends? What? She doesn't have any 'special friends.' In fact, she doesn't have any friends. She never left the house after Izzy died."

"Yes, special friend. She fine, no worry. She go to Dar es Salaam to find you. You rest for night Charlie-boy. You tired. We give food and tomorrow we go find Alex."

CHAPTER THIRTEEN

3 YEARS AGO - IZZY

When the crew made their way down the coast to the ruins early that morning, the excitement in the air was palpable. Rowdy groups split up and placed wagers against each other. By the time they reached the ruins, the anticipation lay thick in the air. They fervently prepared and unpacked their kits with great expectation of this being the day they finally found Rhapta.

"The tide is coming in so, if all goes well, we should be set up and ready when the water is high. Are you sure you got the message to the divers?"

"A hundred percent Mum. They sent word back to meet them here at the site. The divers are coming fully kitted and prepared for the worst. I'm sure they should be here any moment."

"That's great sweets, let's just hope the cave is accessible. The samples I took and tested last night came up positive for sulfur which means it's highly likely we have a cave down there."

"So is that a good thing or a bad thing? Sulfur in the cave that is."

"Well, I know from my research that when sulfur is present, it is most likely an indication of there being blind shafts and higher maze passages. If this is the case, then the chances are there would be large chambers too, and that means it is without a doubt a sunken city. Given all these assumptions are in fact proven, then it further proves that there was quite possibly a collapse of some kind of structure. Whether it was indeed Rhapta remains to be seen, but this is a great day in history one way or another."

"This is super exciting, Mum! I just wish Dad were here to experience this with us."

"Knowing your Dad he has already felt it in his bones."

It was a good thing the divers arrived, or they would still be doubled over with laughter by sunset. Izzy did miss Charles, but somehow, after a lifetime of depending on him, her newfound independence had brought about some liberation of sorts. She was doing this on her own. How many female archaeologists could say that?

"Ma'am, we're going to need you to stand back, please, for our safety and yours. We will be fastening our guide ropes, and our ground crew will be watching everything on the monitors from up here. You're welcome to join them but, in the event of an explosion or a collapse, it is best to keep a safe distance."

Izzy was a get-in-and-get-dirty kind of woman. She detested standing back, but she respected the divers' skill and complied.

"Sure thing, I'll have my crew explore a bit further inland if that's okay? How long will the dive take though?" Trying not to tap her foot impatiently.

"It's hard to tell Ma'am. It all depends on what we find down there. If all goes well, our initial exploration will be about two hours. Our tanks don't allow for more. Once the first dive team is up, I'll send down the second for another two-hour session. Anything beyond that we would have to wait until tomorrow before we dive again."

There was a deadline and impending greed hot on her heels, not to mention they had been at it for decades and the excitement was too much for them all to bear. She was certain that by now the word of having found a possible underground cave and ruins was all over the country. It wouldn't take long for the treasure hunters to show up and stake their claim.

"I understand. The divers run the risk of getting the bends."

"What's that?" Alex asked.

"It's decompression illness from being under the water too long with the oxygen tanks," the diver replied.

Conceding to not have any other choice but to practice patience, Izzy turned to look for Eric whom again, was nowhere in sight. It was now a regular occurrence and shouldn't seem strange, but it was.

"How is it that guy is always missing? Just what in heavens' name is that boy up to? When he surfaces, I'm not taking my eyes off that redhead, IF he surfaces."

It was no secret that she was annoyed. She tried her best to push the nagging feeling in her gut away by busying herself with pitching the tents. Alexandra was behind her laptop doing more research as was usual. She had a mind like a sponge and questioned everything. Took after her Dad that was certain.

"Can you tear yourself away for a little walk? I want to see what's behind those trees over there."

"Sure Mum, I'll bring our kit just in case. There's not much we can do here except wait. We'll have to let the divers do their thing and come back later."

"You're a chip off the old block my girl."

They zigzagged through the rows of palm trees in search of any possible clues or evidence pointing to the existence of a lost civilization. A couple of hours inland and the tropical paradise coast disappeared into a yellow Savannah with

Acacia trees and ferocious predators. One would never guess the ocean surrounded all of that wildlife.

Loose coconuts and rotten mangos lay scattered on the ground everywhere. It was an island paradise. Large boulders and palm leaves were scattered throughout the treed floor. It was a perpetual tourist hotspot for the sun seekers. Nearby Zanzibar Island was one of the most sought-after holiday destinations in Africa. Izzy took it all in. What's not to like? It looked like a postcard.

"Did you bring the puzzle box and the scroll sweetheart? Can we sit down here for two minutes and have another look? I think we're missing something."

It was a silly question. Alexandra slept with it every night. Of course, she would have it with her. She hadn't parted with it since they found it.

"Okay, let's go through all this again, shall we? We have a wooden puzzle box that delivered a secret scroll with a seal. The seal has the numbers 11-5-25 on which spells the word KEY in English. The scroll has a clue written in black cursive to which the answer simply is, *a river*, and all this was safely locked away in a clever combination box. What am I missing?"

"Nothing Mum. That's pretty much it."

"And you are certain the cipher is translating to English, and the word KEY is the only possible answer?"

"Yip. Pretty sure. I tried many other options, but none worked. Dad agreed."

"Could it be that the box has another puzzle in it maybe? Perhaps something else is hidden in it?"

"I don't think so. I mean I was at it for hours. Unless it has two hidden drawers."

She started fiddling with it again. Turning this way and that, slipping latches in and out and still nothing.

"And the knife? Did we inspect that thoroughly?"

"I believe so yes, Dad did."

"Let's have another look there too. We found both in practically the same quadrant, so perhaps it's linked somehow."

Izzy turned the knife over and inspected it from all angles. She followed suit with the box and the scroll. It all looked very straightforward. Nothing different from what they had already found and decrypted.

"Fancy a coconut while we work Mum? Might as well make a decent picnic of it," laughing at herself for being so goofy. Alex picked up the coconut and walked to a nearby rock to crack open the coconut but suddenly stopped.

"Mum, I think you'd better come look at this."

Izzy turned to look where her daughter stood bent over an oblong rock-like object.

"What? It's a rock. Bigger than normal but still, just a rock."

"Uhm no, I don't think so."

Alex had her mother's curiosity piqued, and she strolled over nevertheless, still enamored with the knife.

"I've never seen anything like it. It looks like a... NO! It simply isn't possible! There is just no way this is a—"

"Are you thinking what I'm thinking Mum?" Alex interrupted.

"I never thought I would see the day Alexandra, but yes. It looks a lot like a prehistoric egg!"

"Yip! That's what I was thinking exactly. It's enormous. What type of bird lays a gray egg this size?" She paused and added.

"I'm going to touch it."

"NO! Don't Alexandra! If it belongs to the bird I'm thinking of then this could not have good consequences at all! Let's just leave it here, for now, mark the location and come back later with the crew. We would need to take all precautions. It could be alive, so we will need to run some tests first."

"What? Are we just going to leave it here? That's crazy, Mum."

But before the two could enter into a disagreement, they heard a shrill shrieking sound followed by a thunderous bellow that literally shook the trees around them.

"That's not a Hadeda nor thunder Mum! Look up!"

Izzy's heart stopped, and in no time the hair on her neck stood up.

"Run Alexandra! Run!"

Fear gripped her every cell as she grabbed a still gawking Alexandra by the hand and ran as fast as her two legs could carry her. The thick sand made it hard to run in and her leg muscles burned under the strain. She secretly longed for Charles to come to their rescue.

So much for her independence, she thought. Alexandra swooshed past her. She was as swift as a gazelle. Izzy looked up to find the massive bird swoop in over them, just missing Izzy's shoulder by fractions. The force of its wings knocked her off balance, and she tripped and fell flat on her face in the sand.

Surrounded by abundant vegetation and mango trees, she jumped to her feet and sidestepped behind the closest tree to find her bearings. She looked across to Alexandra where she too had found cover behind a tree. Izzy's eyes were franticly searching for a way out. As her eyes skimmed over her surroundings she realized the vegetation was entirely flattened.

"Alexandra, look around us! We're in the middle of her nest!"

Human remains lay scattered all around them. Skeletons, skulls, and several half-eaten animal carcasses were strewn across the sandy floor. Izzy was right. They were smack bang caught in the middle of her lair and they were trapped.

"We need to get out of here Mum or we will be this creature's next snack!"

The bird turned and came back around, taking another dive straight toward them. Its pelican-like beak was monstrous. Its bright volcanic red body was as stealth as a Navy airplane. Her razor sharp claws were the size of six sickles bundled together. It was unlike anything Izzy or Alex had ever seen and resembled something from the Jurassic age. Or perhaps it was from the pits of hell.

"We need to run back to the beach Alexandra. There's nowhere else to run to. If we run from tree to tree, skipping about three at a time, we could make our way out bit by bit. You can get a head start, and I'll cover you with the rifle. I am not taking any chances here today. Curse or no curse."

"Okay, load it up. I'm ready Mum."

The giant bird sensed their plan and swooped low to scoop Izzy up with its claws. She missed her by a fraction as Izzy twirled her body around the back of the tree-trunk.

"NOW!" She shouted to Alexandra as the bird gained height to turn and come back for another dive.

The crushing sound of carcasses under their feet was revolting, but the pair both made it unscathed to the next tree. Just in time too as the bird came in for another dive. This time aiming for Alexandra. Izzy cocked her rifle, grateful for having the foresight to bring it. Aiming she shot off one bullet at it. But she missed and cursed the creature. It looked straight at her. The shot made her angry and it sent off another shrill sound in warning before ascending for another dive.

"NOW!" Izzy shouted at Alex again.

They ran and cleared another four trees. The bird was relentless and dived down again. Izzy aimed the rifle at it once more and pulled the trigger. Somehow the bullet clipped its wing and tipped it off balance, but the bird quickly recovered and swooped past her again for another ascent.

"NOW!" This time it was Alexandra shouting.

They ran again having now completed most of the tree-to-tree relay around its lair. They were almost in the clear. Perhaps, with any luck, the bird will give up once they were out of the den and no longer a threat to her. Izzy looked back preparing herself for the bird to dive at them again but it was gone.

"Can you see it?" She shouted across to Alexandra.

"No, I think she's gone, Mum."

"I doubt that. It is lurking about here somewhere. If we run now we are an open target."

"You clipped it with that last shot. Perhaps it's dead."

They listened for any sound of its wings, nothing. Dead silence. It was too big for it not to be seen. They were so close to the beach.

"Let's make a run for three more trees, Mum! I don't see how we have any other options here. We can hardly hang about here all day. Sooner or later it will win if we stick around."

"Okay, on three again....ONE...TWO...THREE!"

Again they sprinted to their next beacon that was outside of its lair, and Izzy looked back to Alexandra as she passed her second tree. Behind her, coming from her right, the bird was in full flight and came straight for her.

"INCOMING THREE O'CLOCK!"

Izzy cocked her rifle, aimed and shot.

"Not on my watch you demon!"

Seconds later the bird hit the tree behind Alexandra and fell to the ground.

"RUN ALEX RUN!"

Too afraid to look back to see if it was dead they made a beeline through the trees in the direction of the beach. Through the first clearing, they heard men's voices and looked up to find Eric with some of the crew, guns loaded, heading straight toward them.

"What's happening? What are you running from?" Eric questioned.

"RUN!" Alex shouted as her and Izzy rushed past him, stopping for the first time when they finally got to the beach safely.

"What the hell was that all about?" Eric, who never saw the bird, asked.

"That was *the* raptor bird, Eric. We accidentally landed in its lair when we went for a walk, and the thing came at us, an enormous beast with fireball eyes and claws and everything!" Alex said trying to catch her breath.

"Nah, that's impossible, everyone knows that's just a story the elders made up to entertain the young ones," Eric said in disbelief.

"Well, we saw it with our very own eyes. It was very real, I assure you. Godzilla would have nothing on this thing. Rotten animal carcasses and human skeletons lay everywhere in its lair. I don't think the ones who came before us were as lucky as us to escape. There were hundreds of bones."

"We have to go back and take some photos. To send to Charles of course. He's going to want to see this, I'm sure." All of a sudden Eric's curiosity piqued.

Izzy finally spoke. "Be my guest, Eric. Just don't expect us to go back there with you. You'll be dead in seconds."

"But Charles has to see for himself," he continued planting suspicion in Izzy's mind over why he wanted to go back there so badly.

"Do you have a death wish or something? Trust me, Eric, it doesn't matter. I can put together a couple of rough sketches for him. That thing is etched in my mind forever, believe me," Alex warned.

"I'd listen to her if I were you, Eric. That demonic creature is nothing but trouble. It will rip you to shreds," Izzy added.

Not wanting to argue with him any further she pushed him aside and walked over to the scuba divers who came out from their first dive already. If he was going to be stupid enough to walk straight into a death trap, then so be it. He was warned.

"And? What does it look like down there? Anything we can work with?" Izzy turned her attention to the divers.

"Ma'am, it was amazing. There are a series of underwater chambers and tunnels of which we haven't seen half. It is simply spectacular. The second crew is down there now collecting more samples and taking photos. We rigged it up with the surveillance cameras already. Come see."

The monitors displayed perfect underwater images of the crew collecting samples. The crew leader fiddled with a couple of buttons and zoomed several cameras in on the map of tunnels spread out beneath the surface.

"These edges here are what protrude above the water at low tide. They are the outer edges of the tunnels, not structures. There is some sulfur but not too much to jeopardize the dive. We should know more once the second team is up."

"Have you found any objects of any kind? Any relics whatsoever?"

"We did lift a couple of wine goblets and some porcelain plates, yes ma'am. I suspect the glasses quite possibly have copper or brass stems. It's not gold but to be sure, we're soaking it in the tank over there. And then one or two objects that we aren't quite sure of what it is yet. It could be knives or swords, so we put them in the electrolysis tank. There is quite a bit of erosion and oxidization."

"So then that's proof that it came into contact with dry air at some stage. Perhaps someone found it and threw it back," Izzy interjected.

"No, ma'am, not likely. I think it's more probable that it dislodged at some stage in one of the currents perhaps and floated to the surface during a low tide."

"Sure, that could explain it too yes. Alexandra, get your father on your computer please sweets. We need to let him know what we have all discovered. To gain further clarity it's going to require his expertise for sure."

Izzy dared not mention their narrow escape from the raptor bird in front of the men at this stage. The entire country was aware of the legendary bird of prey that will release the curse of Kifa and devour anything in its path if anyone came near Rhapta. If they heard it actually existed, they will stop the dive, and then they can forget about finding anyone brave enough to go down there again. If she was lucky, she killed it and there's nothing to worry about anyway.

Alex relentlessly tried getting a connection to Charles, but there was interference with the service.

"Leave it, sweetheart. We'll try again later. Eric has gone missing again. You're going to need to use your camera to shoot some images of the artifacts."

CHAPTER FOURTEEN

3 YEARS AGO - IZZY

The divers brought up more artifacts during the afternoon.

"Ma'am, I think you need to have a look at this one. I've never seen anything like it. It's quite corroded, but it looks to be a sign of some sort."

Across from the main diving tent, a sizable crane was in the process of hoisting a somewhat strangely shaped object from the water. Chunks of kelp and seaweed dangled off it, and it was a bit hard to make out exactly what it was while it swiveled from side to side.

"What do you think it is, Mum?"

"It's rather odd looking. I don't have a clue. It looks like a flat object, and yet it has curves and sharp edges. I really can't tell, but I do know it does look strangely familiar."

Alexandra was busy chewing her thumbnail. Something she did whenever she got anxious or impatient. Patience had never been her strong suit. Izzy turned her attention back to the find, which was now almost completely salvaged from the water and took a couple of steps closer to inspect it. They carefully pulled off the shards of seaweed that covered the peculiar object. Bit by bit they discovered the relic wasn't gold or copper. It appeared to be quite rusted and discolored in places. She started taking off scrapings immediately and tested them in their make shift lab. An hour later the results confirmed it was, as she suspected, pure silver.

Izzy and her daughter carefully started cleaning their find which lay flat on a table in front of them. Izzy ran her fingers over the flat surface and outlined the edges with her pen onto the paper underneath it.

"Okay, lift it up please?" She instructed some of the crew.

They stood back a couple of steps to get the full perspective when Alex stopped dead in her tracks and squeezed her mother's hand.

"What's wrong Alex?"

"You mean you can't see it, Mum? Look, look carefully."

Izzy took another couple of paces back and turned her head sideways.

"The bird, it's the raptor bird."

"Yes, it's the shape of the raptor bird that chased us, Mum."

"Okay put it down again please?" Izzy instructed again.

"Wait! Stop!" Alexandra shouted seconds before it hit the table. "Lift it up again!"

"What is it darling?"

"Look here, underneath the wing, there."

In front of their very eyes, underneath the massive bird's wing, was the word RHAPTA.

It took several seconds of complete silence, as they stood stunned, digesting what they had read beneath the wing before the crew broke into jubilant cheers. They danced, clapped hands and jumped up and down with joy. Izzy thought her heart skipped several beats before it finally came to a standstill in her throat.

"Mum, you actually did it. You finally found your Rhapta, for real this time!"

Izzy couldn't react. She could hear the joy in her daughter's voice and the cheering crew behind her, but somehow her emotions were numb. Instead, she heard herself say.

"Alex, get your father on the computer and tell him he needs to get back here right away."

That's all she managed to get out of her now constricted throat. She knew what this meant. Word will get out very quickly, and they would have treasure salvers up in their business before sunset.

"Mum, why aren't you happy? Do you realize what's going on here? You found Rhapta."

She pulled Alexandra aside.

"Please don't get me wrong, sweetheart. I am happy. Of course I'm happy, but we are going to need to be extremely careful now that we have found it. There are a lot of dangerous people after it too. If word lands in the wrong hands they'll be claiming their stake and things could get very ugly. Please get your father on the phone and tell him to get here FAST!"

Alexandra stared at her mother with a stark face. She looked scared and frazzled but Izzy grasped the gravity of the threat this posed.

After another stern nudge she was on the satellite phone, and before long Izzy heard Charles reacting much the same as she did.

"Dad says he's on the next plane out. He should be here by sunrise. What do we do now? Sit on it? It's the best news ever."

"Please try to understand Alexandra. You're going to have to trust me on this one. We need to keep it under wraps as much as possible. Certainly, until your father gets here."

The crew and diving team alike, on the other hand, were in full celebration still gawking over the large crest and two-dozen other relics they had salvaged over the past week. Izzy panicked knowing she'd have to tone the guys down, and quickly. The last thing they now needed was a pack of treasure hunters on their backs. She cleared her throat and gathered them up.

"Guys! Listen up, please? Our excavation is a momentous day in history and I, along with you, are ecstatic that we are finally making headway in our quest for finding Rhapta. I implore you to please practice extreme caution and keep this under wraps. We cannot let word get out just yet. We need to get the right authorities out here and have it documented properly. I don't think I need to remind you that there will be a battle of claim on this salvage. We cannot, I repeat, cannot discuss this with anyone."

Their blank faces stared back at her.

"I have summoned the authorities, and they will be here with Charles by sunrise. We will deploy a search team in the morning for the raptor egg Alexandra, and I found earlier." Izzy masterfully put out this comment for bait before adding. "This mission will not be for the faint-hearted. As some of you might have heard by now, we encountered, what we believe to have been the mythical raptor bird. I did take a shot at it and believe I hit the creature, but there is a chance he might have survived."

A rumbling drifted through the small group.

"In the meantime, let's call it a day and get some much-needed rest. The last couple of weeks have been long. We will assemble and pick it up again in the morning once Charles arrives."

Izzy walked away and reflected on her carefully delivered speech. She knew she was totally dispiriting the crew. She was as elated as her crew was, probably more since she had been looking for Rhapta her entire life, but she couldn't run the risk of getting them all killed. She looked around searching for Eric.

"Alexandra, when last have you seen Eric?"

"Uhm not sure Mum. I'm sure he was around here just now, or perhaps I think when we escaped the bird. Why?"

"Don't you find it strange that he disappears so often? I mean, where the heck does he go?"

"He did say he is dealing with some family issues. Maybe they're not resolved yet."

Another look through their campsite for Eric also turned up empty. Perhaps she was overreacting, and it *was* just family business. She just couldn't convince her senses of that.

"We should get some sleep sweetheart. We might need to face that creature again tomorrow."

It wasn't long before the camp settled down and the night-time sounds filled the air. Alexandra was fast asleep next to her. Izzy was tired too and just started dozing off when she was startled by a noise outside their tent. She sat up in bed, her eyes wide open and her ears turned toward the direction from which it came.

It was just before midnight and Izzy found herself cursing Eric for probably lurking around outside again for a space to sleep. She poked her head outside the tent. It was pitch black. Imminent rain clouds covered the moon, causing there to be hardly any light.

"Eric!" She whisper-shouted but heard no response. She stepped outside and walked around the side of the tent.

"Eric!" She whisper-called again. "Is that you?"

Silence responded. Not a single sound except the lapping of the ocean water onto the rocks. Perhaps it was her imagination. She was practically asleep, so maybe it was the beginning of a dream.

Consoled by the idea that it was probably just her imagination playing wild tricks on her, she turned around to go back inside and, moments before entering the tent, heard a branch break in the trees behind the tent. As she turned to look back at the noise, a large, muscular hand covered her mouth from behind and she was pinned down, face first in the sand. She tried to scream, but her voice strained as they pulled her neck backward. They tied her hands with rope behind her back. Any attempts to wrestle herself free were altogether futile against their brutal force. All she felt were two big men pinning her down on the ground. There was not a word exchanged between them. Complete silence. She tried biting the one man's hand, but it barely had any effect other than prompting them to tape her mouth closed.

"Mum? Is that you?"

The commotion must have woken Alex up. Izzy shut her eyes and stopped wrestling, silently praying, pleading to God to not let Alex come out of the tent. Please don't come out Alex. Stay there, please, she transferred her thoughts.

A few seconds later Alex popped her head out through the side of the tent and shone her bright torchlight directly onto where the men had captured Izzy.

"MUM! NO! LEAVE HER A-L-O-N-E!"

Unable to speak Izzy felt her attackers pull her to her feet and dragged her away between the dense trees behind the tent. Alexandra's eyes, locked on her mother's, were filled with terror. She froze not knowing what to do.

"MUM! STOP! LEAVE HER ALONE! HELP! SOME-BODY HELP!" She screamed over and over.

Izzy tried to dig her heals into the sand in a useless attempt to slow them down. At least until some of the crew hopefully came to her rescue. But her capturers were just too quick and too forceful. She felt a heavy blow to the back of her skull before everything went dark.

CHAPTER FIFTEEN

3 YEARS AGO - ALEX

"Alexandra, slow down honey, please? Tell me slowly now. How many were there? Could you make out any of their faces or anything else that might bear significance to recognizing them?"

"I can't...I don't—"

"It's okay sweetheart. Just take a deep breath and start slowly okay? It's crucial the police get on top of this as soon as possible."

Alex read many a paper in which they said the first forty-eight hours was critical in a kidnapping. The longer they waited to get on the case the more significant the chances were that her mother was—

Alex couldn't get herself to even think the word. She wiped the tears with her already drenched hanky and took a deep breath.

"Maybe two, the men were big and... and they tied her up and—"

The tears ran freely again. Her eyes already hurt from all the crying. Breathe Alex, do this for Mum, she spoke to herself.

"They pulled her in between the trees over there. They took her Dad! What do they want with her?"

"Alexandra, look at me. They took her to find the treasure for them. They need her. She's no good to them if she isn't alive. They won't harm your mother, Alexandra, I assure you. Now think. Can you recall if they resembled anyone we might recognize? What were they wearing?"

Her brain fought back hard not to recall the events. Alex willed it not to conjure up the images that were now etched in her mind forever. But she had to. If they ever wanted to see her mother alive, Alex would have to recall every last detail.

"They were black...and tall and they had black T-shirts and green military pants on. I think they also wore black berets. They didn't speak to each other at all. Almost as if they rehearsed every part of her kidnapping."

Kidnap. The savages her mother had warned her about had kidnapped her mother. It was exactly why she wanted to keep their discovery quiet. Alex felt as if she were in a horrific nightmare. A very, very bad dream. But, when she looked at the five police constables and forensics team scouring the area for any evidence, it became very real.

"That's good honey, what else?"

"Nothing, the men had no guns or knives or anything. Just tied her up and dragged her away."

A vivid image of her mother's eyes flashed before her. "Dad, her eyes, she looked so sad and...desperate. I didn't do anything to help her. I froze! I could have taken her gun and shot them. Instead I did nothing! Jelani ran after them but lost their trail. He must still be somewhere out there looking for her. He hasn't made it back here yet."

"I know darling. Don't worry about Jelani. He'll be fine. If anyone can track them, it would be him. Did they take anything with them? Her bag, journal, anything?"

"No, that is what's so strange. They didn't even try to find the scroll or the box or any of Mum's notes. I still have it with me."

"You do? You have the cipher code and the box and even the knife? They didn't take it?"

"No, look. They never even came into the tent and tried. I sleep with it under my bed."

She pulled out the bag of relics and double-checked. Just to be sure. It was all there. Nothing was missing. Charles was perplexed.

"What does this mean Dad? If they were after the treasure, they would have forced their way into the tent and taken this too. It doesn't make any sense."

"You're right Alexandra, it doesn't. Let's just think for a moment here. They wouldn't need the riddle anymore because we're at the river already. The cipher code is a bunch of numbers to them that your mother has memorized. They're looking for the key. They probably didn't even know we had the relics. I mean, how would they?"

He was right. They wouldn't know of the box and the cipher code or the knife.

"Perhaps word got out through the dive team and all the artifacts they pulled from the site over the last week. It wasn't unlikely that someone blabbed their mouth off during a stupor."

"Do you think they've been watching us here Dad?"

"No way of knowing. What's that?" Charles pointed past her toward their latest find.

They walked over to the table where the massive sign shaped like the raptor bird lay covered under a sheet. In the chaos of the kidnapping, she neglected to show it to him.

"We retrieved this yesterday."

She drew the sheet back and watched her father's face as he read the engraved word.

He drew a sharp breath and yanked the rest of the sheet off.

"Well, I'll be...tell me it is what I think it is."

"It is Dad. Mum and I were walking among the trees yesterday, and we found an enormous egg. Before we knew it, a gigantic raptor bird chased us, and it somehow trapped us in its lair. Dead animals and skeletons lay everywhere. We managed to escape and then the divers found this yesterday."

"And you didn't think to call me and tell me? The relic crest is why they took her! You need to show me where you found the egg. Let's go."

"But Dad, that bird is a killing machine. Mum shot it, but perhaps it survived, and now it's out there waiting for us. Heck there should be more than one otherwise how could she lay an egg?"

"It's a chance we're going to have to take Alexandra. Come on."

Charles had her by the hand as he pulled her toward the trees. His gun was loaded and ready to shoot, and she had her mother's rifle uncomfortably tucked under one arm. Now that she was aware of what lurked between the trees, it felt eerie. Her eyes were peeled for any sign of the bird as they walked deeper in between the trees. There wasn't a normal bird chirping or a crab pushing up between their feet. Like the very life of the area was sucked out into an invisible vacuum.

"Here, the egg was somewhere around here. It looked like a large rock in the shape of a football."

They scoured the area, but there was nothing.

"I don't understand. I know it was right here. We sat under this tree here with the funny looking trunk and then I walked here to crack a coconut. It was here, I'm sure of it."

Doubts filled Alex's mind. She was traumatized so it was possible her memory was skewed. But as she wrestled with her own thoughts and mind, she knew, beyond doubt, that they were on the right spot and that the egg had disappeared.

"Which direction did you run in when the thing was chasing you?"

"That way, its nest is over there. Dad, I don't think this is a good idea. How are we supposed to help Mum if we both end up dead?"

"We're not going to die, sweetheart, not today."

He seemed very sure of himself. She's never had any reason to doubt him in the past. He was fully aware of what he was doing.

They set off toward the lair and it wasn't long before they hit its perimeter. Alex watched as her father paused to get a mental hold of the multitude of half eaten animals and human skeletons that lay scattered throughout.

"This is it, Dad. The bird attacked us, and we ran from tree to tree back to the beach."

"Is this all you found? Nothing else?"

"Nothing else. We didn't have much time to explore any further because the bird chased us."

"You did great my darling. I'm going to need you to put some sketches together so we can try to find out a bit more about what this creature is and how it got here. For now, let's head back and see what the police might have found. Perhaps Jelani is back too."

B ut, two weeks later their investigation still turned up empty. The trail had run dead and Jelani returned with nothing. The police gave up their investigation and had not one single clue whatsoever. No idea who took Izzy, much less where she was.

"Alexandra, please eat something. They're all doing what they can. We have to trust that they'll find something sooner or later. Don't give up!"

Alex couldn't eat or sleep. Her mother had been kidnapped. Somewhere out there, the rebels had her or, killed her already. Their camp was at the river exactly where they took her in the hope that somehow their daily searches between the trees yielded something.

"Sir, we have word. Please come with me."

Alex startled as the police officer arrived with an envelope in hand.

"What is it Dad? A ransom note."

Charles ripped the envelope open and fell onto the soft sand all the while still staring blankly at the piece of paper in his hand.

"Dad? What's it saying?"

She couldn't bring herself to ask the question but she could tell from his eyes that this was not a ransom note. The tears rolled down his cheeks, as he looked his daughter in the eye.

"She's gone Alexandra. She's gone."

Alex felt her heart being clawed out from her aching chest. Like someone had rammed their fist into her chest and ripped it out with their bare hands. She took the yellowed piece of paper from her father's shaking hands. It was a letter from the authorities.

'*—Her body was found in the nearby rebel camp*' were the only words her eyes extracted from the two short paragraphs. Next to her, her father shook uncontrollably. She had never seen him cry before, ever.

T he weather in London was quite aptly miserable and bitterly cold. Izzy's memorial was as dreary as the weather. Students from Charles' classes and the entire faculty were huddled together under their black umbrellas behind the casket. Their incessant crying and nose blowing irritated Alex. They barely knew her mother. Alex, on the other hand, hadn't shed a single tear since they arrived back home. Even though she tried. She couldn't cry. Like her emotions were ripped along with her heart. She was numb inside, a body without a soul. Home didn't even feel like home anymore.

Someone blowing their nose behind her jerked her thoughts back to the priest who had broken into a poor rendition of Amazing Grace and soon the funeral goers behind her joined in. Her mother hated that song. It was the funeral go-to everyone got, the standard hymn along with the standard bouquet. Izzy Hunt was everything but ordinary.

CHAPTER SIXTEEN

CHARLES

"How you feel dis morning Charlie-boy? You better?"

"Slept for the first time in a long time thank you, Chief. My bones ache, but I feel good."

"Ha, them bones from too old. Your feet good to walk? You go to find Lakicia now. I find new Jeep, and I send my warrior to take you to edge. Come, we eat to make strong."

The chief was a good man who stuck to his promise. Before he knew it, Charles sat in a Jeep the chief traded for fifteen cows.

"I don't know how I can ever repay you for looking after my family Chief. Thank you."

"You go to find Rhapta and Lakicia, Charlie-boy then no curse come. You stop the curse of Kifa and big man-eater bird. No treasure hunter must find first okay? You stop curse over Tanzania people. You do that, I happy."

His English wasn't perfect but Charles understood every word of his plea. He lost his wife and his son, and somehow he thought it was all linked to the curse of Kifa. What exactly the curse was or did, no one knew but they certainly weren't prepared to find out either. The people believed it involved witches and evil spirits and if the ancestors' graves were disturbed and their treasures stolen, it would bring about unspeakable torture and death. There were many who claimed they had seen the massive raptor bird fly over Mafia Island late at night trying to prevent Rhapta from being found. Some say it happened only when treasure hunters came too close.

"You no mess with gods Charlie-boy. You bring curse on people. Rhapta stay sleep. No wake."

"I'll do my best Chief. I give you my word. If I find Rhapta, then it will be declared a historical monument, and no one will be permitted to go there. It could open up infinite and fragile clues of ancient cultures and lost civilizations and reveal important links to the past. And IF there is in fact treasure, the president will claim it, and all this can be put to rest once and for all, but first things first though. I have to find my daughter first."

. . .

The chief had said Alex and Sam headed to the safe house. That made Charles proud. His daughter was sharp as a tack thinking that he'd go there.

He stopped at the edge of the city and slipped on the kaftan the chief gave him as disguise. That was his first time in a dress, and though it was uncomfortable, he was grateful nonetheless. He looked in the Jeep's mirror. The turban wasn't perfectly wrapped but it did the trick. Enough to hide him from the rebels, at least.

The Jeep also blended perfectly with the city's vehicles. It seemed to be what most people used. Satisfied he was now operating incognito he drove towards the safe house. The town was a hustle and bustle of tourists this time of year, and the traffic on the rural roads was enough to drive anyone mad. As he parked around the back of the safe house he noticed the motorcycle the chief gave Alex and Sam to use. They were still there. Delighted she remembered the protocol, he parked alongside it and walked around the block to the entrance.

The rhinoceros door knocker was a welcome sight and he quickly clicked his way through the sequence, all the while looking over his shoulder to be sure he was still alone. Click, click and click. The door opened. It was quiet inside and he stealthily moved to the safety spot under the stairs. He lingered there to listen for voices.

There wasn't the slightest of noises. It was way too quiet for them to be up there. But he was one hundred percent positive it was their motorcycle. Besides, she parked it in precisely the place where he had trained her to. It was also an unspoken signal to announce their presence inside the safe house. But even with that knowledge, Charles wasn't satisfied everything was in order. He took out his gun from under the dress. How women moved around in a dress, was a mystery to him.

There was still no sign of anyone inside. He climbed the staircase, purposefully skipping numbers three and eight, being the creaking ones—another one of his tactics he had set in place as an early warning system. At the top of the stairs, he paused and listened again. He heard a man's voice he didn't quite recognize. Could it be the doctor she was with? There was something so familiar about it though, but it was just too soft to distinguish correctly. He should climb up into the roof and look through the trusses first, to be safe. His fingers reached up into the thin crevice to the right of the door, and he pulled down the lever that released the hidden shaft from the wall. Crawling in on all fours was a tight squeeze and he barely fit; glad he had the foresight to take the dress off before he went in.

The shaft was an old air duct he had built into the wall at a steady incline toward the roof. Izzy never thought it would have any use. But here he was, albeit that the initial purpose was really for it to act as an escape should the door be locked from the outside. Up or down it served a goal.

One, which was undoubtedly coming in quite handy at that moment.

Once at the top he carefully slid aside the small wooden slider to reveal a tiny peephole that allowed a view down into the room.

And what he saw almost stopped his heart. Eric was walking back and forth to the window, gun in hand. Charles strained his neck to get a better angle. He blinked twice, squinting he lay eyes on Alex sitting tied up on the floor. She appeared to be asleep.

Behind her a man sat with his back against hers, also bound and asleep. Concluding it was the doctor behind her his mind raced with questions. His eyes trailed back across the room to where Eric was now talking to someone but from that angle, Charles couldn't see who. Charles shifted his body in the duct and pinned his face against the opening. It was at that moment a heavy feeling punched him right in the stomach. Charles choked back the sobs that threatened to expose his position. His muscles stiffened as he realized it wasn't a dream or hallucination. His chest burned and he struggled to hold back his tears. He looked again. It was her, his darling Izzy. She was alive, gagged and tied up too. Disbelief, shock and anger flooded his emotions all at once and he swore heavily under his breath. It didn't take a genius to put two and two together. Eric had been behind it. HE was the traitor. Izzy was right about that boy all along. 'Never trust a redhead.' How was it that he was so blinded by this man?

As a million questions drowned his mind, Charles tried to contain his trembling body. It took every ounce of willpower not to blow down the door and pounce on Eric, but he needed to keep his wits about him. His daughter and wife who was very much alive was in there with him. If he missed his mark it would blow his chance of getting them out alive. His mind raced as he tried to come up with a plan. It was only Eric, as far as he could tell and he wasn't the most athletically built opponent. He could easily take him. It was four against one of him. If the doctor had any backbone, he would show his worth and pull through for them.

Charles quietly closed the peephole and slowly slid back down the shaft. *Think Charles. You've seen enough movies to think of something here. Think James Bond. What would Bond do?* But the feeble thoughts of imitating his tv hero was soon dismissed as reality sunk in. He wasn't in a movie. This was real life and getting distracted with a make believe character would prove foolish. And, in a single moment of clarity it dawned on him. He needed to distract Eric. Distraction was a perfect plan.

Charles's lacerated feet still ached as he skillfully made his way back down the stairs in search of something that might work as a distraction. There was an old elevator shaft around the back of the building. He had no question in his mind that it would make a racket when he put it into motion and he needed exactly that to be loud enough to lure Eric out. Once he was at the bottom of the stairs, he'd pounce on him and knock him out with his gun. But the old elevator's noise wouldn't be enough. He needed to jar the shaft for extra effect.

A pile of junk lay in the furthermost corner of the safe house. If Eric was watching the surveillance monitors he might spot Charles running across the room. He remembered that Eric stood at the window so perhaps the coast was clear and he could take the chance.

The rubble on the floor yielded nothing except paper and shards of fabric. His mind recalled the pantry. He yanked the doors open and was surprised to see the stockpile of tins pretty much depleted. They must have been there all along. But a couple of tins of beans and some cleaning detergent wouldn't have any effect on his plan. There was another downstairs closet with the mops and brooms. Deciding that would be perfect and that he'd find something there for sure he moved to the closet.

Minutes later Charles managed to tie the broom and mop sticks across the elevator doors, which he wagered everything on to make enough noise to cause a distraction when the elevator moved up and down. Whether it would result in being loud enough he wasn't sure but it was at least a plan. He'd have about ten seconds to run to the stairs, maybe less.

He cursed James Bond for getting inside his head. Charles Hunt was too old for maneuvers like these but it was the only shot he had and he had to at least try.

But he took a deep breath and pushed the button. The elevator was old and probably hadn't worked for years. The loud clanging noise was deafening. Had he known the screeching noise would have been sufficient he wouldn't have even bothered with the brooms.

The ten seconds of running with his injured feet seemed more like ten minutes, but he got under the stairs and waited. His heart beat like loud drums in his chest and he couldn't feel his legs. He prayed Eric was alone and that he didn't have someone else around. As he waited he reasoned that Eric had his wife locked up in there all this time, letting them all believe she was dead. And his abduction? The little weasel was probably behind that too. His own assistant was nothing but a traitor.

His gun was cocked and in position, just incase he got shot at. The elevator was making a loud racket, and he was in position, but Eric took forever to come down the stairs.

"Come on Eric you traitor," he said under his breath and just then heard the lock click on the door above his head. It worked. A sudden coldness hit his core. The dress! He had left it on the stairs. There was no way Eric would miss it. Heck, he had probably stepped on it already.

His eyes followed Eric's feet coming down the stairs, step by step. Charles rolled his tongue through his dry mouth and he needed to swallow but he dared not make a sound. He barely breathed by the time Eric had reached the bottom of the stairs. Doubt suddenly filled his mind, regretted that he was foolish to take matters into his own hands. He should have just called the police instead. Eric was half his age and not recovering from an abduction like he was. But he braved up psyching his mind into teaching the traitor what a real man was made of.

Charles patiently watched as Eric was about to turn the corner where Charles would then clamber him. Unexpectedly the shrill ring of Eric's cell phone shrieked through the warehouse.

"Hello? Yes, I've got them. All except the old man but he could be dead by now. I'll wait for your signal."

Eric hung up and walked to the front door dismissing the distraction as noises caused by the old building's structure. The elevator had reached the top and the clanging noise had already stopped.

Charles needed a plan B and before he could stop himself, bravery got the better of him and he jumped out from behind the stairs.

"Drop your gun, Eric!"

Surprised, Eric spun around, startled by Charles being there and fired a bullet off in his direction. It missed him, just.

"You good-for-nothing traitor! I said drop the gun!" Charles yelled.

Eric fired another bullet at Charles sending him to run for cover behind a steel cupboard.

"There's no point old man. I got your entire family up there. You're not walking out of here alive. Give it up. If we all work together, we can split the bounty."

Over his dead body, Charles thought. Eric wouldn't hesitate to kill the lot of them once they find Rhapta.

"Come out Charles. While you still have a chance. Or else I'll kill them one by one."

He wouldn't, Charles thought. He needed all of them together to decipher the codes. He was bluffing. Besides he needed the box with the scroll and the code. Maybe he hadn't figured that part out yet.

"Okay, Professor. You asked for it. Who will it be first? Your beloved Alex or perhaps the long-lost Izzy? Wouldn't you want just one last moment with her before she dies, again?"

Eric belted out a sadistic laugh, and Charles, who was still hidden behind the cupboard, listened as Eric climbed the stairs.

"Fine! You win Eric."

Charles tucked his gun in the back of his pants and came out with his hands in the air.

"There you are, old man. I knew you'd give in. You're a wimp. I knew you wouldn't let your family die. Slide over your gun, slowly."

"If it's the last thing I do Eric. I'll make you pay for this."

"Give it a rest Charlie. You're done bossing me around. I've been by your side all this time and never once got any claim to any of the relics you've found."

"So that's it then, the fame and fortune? You're no different from all those other treasure hunters Eric. Just after your fifteen-seconds of fame and a briefcase full of money. What about the history?"

"Oh history schmistory. Spare me the theatrics, old man. Who cares if there are hidden civilizations and ancient clay pots? It's all rubbish. What, so it can stand looking pretty in a museum somewhere? No Siree, I am making my own history. I'm tired of doing your dirty work for you, and you take all the credit on the covers of every science publication. And don't even get me started on what people pay to get their hands on artifacts. That in itself is worth it."

"How long Eric? How long have you known Izzy was alive?"

He rendered a disgusting laugh and Charles fought the urge to punch his face in.

"It was you all along, wasn't it Eric? You were the one who told them where the village was."

"You didn't know Professor? The great Professor Charles Hunt couldn't figure it out. You stupid old fool. I had your precious Izzy here all this time. She was my prisoner. Locked up in your steel castle. You're such an idiot. You never once thought of even going to the morgue to see her body, just blindly believed the authorities. They're all in my back pocket old man. We tracked the village through your stupid watch you idiot. We've been digging on Mafia Island since then."

"So all this and you still haven't found Rhapta. Well, isn't that funny? It doesn't exist you, birdbrain. Let me guess, you haven't found anything, and now you need me, and the wooden box, don't you?"

"So then you do have it. Where's the key old man?"

"If you kill me or any of my family up there you'll never get it, mark my words."

"Then I guess we're all going treasure hunting together aren't we? Get up there to your precious family. Move it!"

What should have been a feeling of walking the gallows up the stairs, was instead squelched by sheer excitement. At the top of those stairs his beloved Izzy and Alex would be waiting. The thought of seeing Izzy again propelled Charles up the stairs with skill and speed.

"Izzy!" He ran over to where she was bound and gagged on the floor and pulled the cloth from her mouth.

"It's you, my love. All this time, I never knew."

"Easy there Professor. Don't even think about untying her. Put the gag back in her mouth. NOW!"

His fingers fumbled with the gag around her neck, but Charles did as Eric instructed. Only, he loosened it a little.

"Sorry, my love. I'll get us out of here and this time, you're going home."

"Dream on old man. Like hell she is. None of you are going home or have you forgotten you're helping me find that treasure?" He shoved Charles down onto the floor.

He looked across to Alexandra who just woke from all the ruckus. There wasn't a tear in her eyes. Instead, a bland look of disbelief lay on her face as she stared into her mother's eyes for the first time since she was captured years ago.

"Sweetheart, it's true. Your mother is alive. This double-crosser had her locked up here all these years. You'll be okay my sweets. Hang in there."

"Shut up old man, or I'll gag you too."

Eric would have done that already if he wanted to. For some reason, he hadn't tied or gagged Charles yet who winked at his daughter. Alex nodded her head in response, her eyes now pooled with tears.

"It's okay sweetheart. We'll figure this out."

"Yeah yeah, that's enough of this soppy hogwash. Go sit down and put your hands behind your back."

So much for not tying his hands, Charles thought and followed his backstabbing assistant's orders again, flinching as the ropes hurt when Eric tightened it around his wrists.

"Who are you waiting for, Eric? Who's in it with you? They're using you, you know? Once they arrive, they'll kill you. Think about it. They won't need you anymore."

"Shut up! Who cares what you think?"

"You should Eric. How much time do you have before they get here? I have a Jeep parked out back. Help us get out and find Rhapta, and we'll make sure you claim the discovery and the uni's reward."

Charles could see Eric's birdbrain ticking away as he contemplated the temptation.

"Come on Eric. You know I'm good for it. I give you my word. This is what you've always wanted, isn't it? To claim fame and fortune. Well, here's your chance. We can do it together. You let us free and you can take it all."

Eric pointed the gun at Alexandra's head.

"I'll kill her first old man. You mess with me, and I'll kill her. Do you get me?"

Charles merely nodded. He was in luck. The naive fool took the bait. They would find a way of escaping and if Eric as much as hurt a hair on Izzy and Alex's heads Charles would personally gut him.

"Get up, all of you and give me the keys to the Jeep."

Charles tossed them over.

CHAPTER SEVENTEEN

THE HUNT

"Drive old man, and don't even think of trying any funny business. You three shut your mouths and put your hands up against the bull bar. Tie them up, Doc and make sure those knots are tight."

They did as Eric instructed even though hatred was on all their tongues.

Alex looked over at her mother who sat quietly next to her. Her hair was messy and her clothes dirty. Her arms showed signs of old scars and fresh bruising. It was evident they had been torturing her? She looked exhausted and broken, almost in a trance. She lay her head on Izzy's shoulder. She still couldn't believe her mother was alive. All this time they thought she was dead and she wasn't.

She was very much alive and held prisoner by a traitor in their midst.

"Where do you want me to drive to Eric?" Charles asked mockingly.

"Where do you think old man? The river mouth of course. Hope you brought your goggles. We're going to do a bit of diving."

"Diving? We can't dive. Those caves are dangerous, and if the tide is not in, it will be impossible to do," Charles exclaimed suddenly shaking.

Sam turned sideways and looked at Alex with disbelief. He had overcome many a fear on this journey, but diving was not something he looked forward to. Alex wished she could tell him not to worry and that they'd think of something to escape it, but her mouth was still gagged. Instead, she reassured him with her eyes and hoped he understood.

Forty minutes later, with Eric's gun still pointed at Charles' head, the captured party arrived at the spot by the river mouth, the exact place from which her mother had been kidnapped all those years before. Had she not been alive there would be no way on earth Alex would ever set foot there again, but there she was, squashed next to her in the back of a hijacked Jeep looking more nervous the nearer they got.

Charles' eyes sought out his daughter's through the rearview mirror. He was trying to tell her something. Alex caught on and replied in silence through her frowning eyes. In return Charles cast his eyes up to the sky. Alex knew exactly that her father was hinting toward the raptor bird. She got it, so she blinked slowly in confirmation.

Eric untied Sam's hands and instructed him to leave the others tied up. He was under the impression Sam was the least threat to him. Little did he know how far he had come on this journey.

"Now get out and start walking to the beach."

Alex cleared her throat to get his attention and pushed out some muffled sounds from underneath the gag.

"What do you want Agoraphobe?"

Alex narrowed her eyes. If one thing was clear, then it was that she had long since passed the time where she carried that label. No one called her that and got away with it. But this was not the time for revenge. The time would come for that and he'd regret his words. She spoke through the gag again.

Eric stared her down in irritation but succumbed and yanked the rag from her mouth.

"Spit it out daddy's girl. What do you want?"

Her knuckles pushed through her skin at Eric's taunting as she fought back the urge to head-butt his red freckled nose flat against his face. But her father's eyes cautioned her not to. With her mouth free she spoke with confidence. "Why would you want to dive if you can access the cave from out here?" She nodded her head toward the trees.

"Aah, so you've been holding out on me after all? What are you waiting for then you little brat? Start walking."

Charles smiled with his eyes as he took pride in his daughter's smarts. Sam, on the other hand, frowned with confusion. He was in the dark over their historical encounter with the bird. She mouthed for him to trust her during a brief moment when Eric's back was turned towards them.

The trees were far denser than three years ago and Alex paused to make sure she was going the right way. She recognized the trees leading up to the edge of the bird's lair. They were very close and she kept her eyes open for any signs of the raptor bird. Under normal circumstances, she would have prayed the creature would stay away, but now, now she needed this bird to come to their rescue.

"Why are you stopping? Keep moving!" Eric shouted from the back.

He was at the back of the line as Alex led them through the trees, his gun wedged firmly into Izzy's back.

Come on bird! Where are you? Alex silently called out to it. Up ahead she saw remnants of a fresh carcass and inconspicuously turned to look at her parents behind her. They both noticed it, and Sam astutely caught on that something was about to happen. Eric, totally oblivious to the fact that he was about to face death, kicked a coconut sideways, like he was trying to score a goal.

Alex thought him to be a complete idiot. She was sure whoever he was in cahoots with had by now already discovered they were not at the safe house anymore. Either way, Eric was dead.

But the bird was nowhere to be seen. Alex turned and looked at her mother in question. Izzy shrugged her shoulders ever so slightly. Perhaps she did kill it that day? But further along their walk through the trees there was another fresh carcass and they instantly knew the creature was still very much alive.

"Where is it, brat? All I see are dead animals everywhere. If you're taking me on a wild goose chase I'm going to cut your tongue out, do you hear me?"

"And that will get you closer to finding Rhapta for sure, won't it you fool?" She lashed out in response.

"So, you still have that little attitude of yours is it? I don't scare that easily woman. Now where are we going?"

Alex pushed her chin toward the trees further ahead. Eric scanned the direction she pointed out and found nothing. Within a second he was behind her and yanked her head back by her hair.

"There's nothing! You're lying!"

"No! I'm not. It's been a while, okay? The vegetation has changed. Perhaps it's a little bit off this way."

Of course she was lying. She was trying to buy them more time. It was just about sunset so they'd have to wait until the morning if it got too dark. Perhaps then they would have an opportunity to escape during the night.

Eric's phone echoed through the trees and she watched his face drain from red to pale white. If his accomplices found him out now they'd kill him, and them.

"What are you staring at, brat? You have exactly five minutes to find that cave entrance or I'll kill this boyfriend of yours." He ejected a ball of saliva at Sam's feet.

Her eyes met Sam's who, strangely enough rolled his eyes, making it understood that he wasn't intimidated. He didn't seem worried in the least. He was a good head and shoulders taller than Eric and certainly more athletic in build, so perhaps he saw him not to be a threat.

Her father, on the other hand, might not be in such a good position to wrestle him off if he went for him. He looked as battered and exhausted as her mother. She couldn't risk losing any of them, so she decided to turn to the right and walk towards the bird's lair. It was time to pull out all the stops.

As they came closer, the bird's powerful wings flapped above their heads. The bird rushed up from the side and announced her presence with a shrill shriek so loud it pushed them all to the ground. Charles grabbed the opportunity and kicked at Eric's face, rendering him lights out next to a bare carcass. With their hands still tied behind their backs and their mouths gagged, they each headed for cover behind a tree. Using the razor sharp edges of the palm tree, Alex cut through the thin ropes and freed her hands.

"Use the tree to cut your ropes!" She yelled across to the others.

She watched as Sam ran through the lair towards her mother to untie her hands, momentarily causing her to hold her breath. But he made it and freed Izzy's hands.

"Dad, are you okay?"

"All good here Alex. Now what?"

The bird turned and dived down to where Eric still lay passed out in the sand. Its gigantic claws clutched Eric's unconscious body and ascended above the trees. There was no saving him now. They needed to save themselves.

"Guys, I think I see a hollow in the bushes, look. Over there! We can hide in it! Let's make a run for it before the bird turns around again," Alex called out.

"Okay, let's do it and hope the shelter is large enough for all of us!" Charles shouted back.

"It looks fine Dad, come. On three okay?" Looking across to her mother and Sam where they waited on her count.

She counted it down and Alex pushed herself away from the tree trunk sprinting across the lair, crushing several skeleton bones under her feet. She briefly looked back to see the monster bird dipping low for another dive. Her foot hit the remains of a dead animal or something, and she fell flat on her face next to it. Bewildered she looked up to see the rest of the group all safely inside the hollow, shouting for her to get up.

Her hand sank inside the rotten animal's carcass as she pushed herself up. It was disgusting but she sprinted for the hollow and got to it split seconds ahead of the bird who came in for another dive. Izzy pulled her in by her arm with a strength she didn't know she possessed. Before she knew it, she had Alex soundly in front of a wall of hanging tree roots. The raptor, apparently upset by the party making it to the opening, swooshed overhead and turned to come in from a different angle. Dead ahead the raptor made a clear descent straight toward them.

Its sharp beak was open and ready to devour anything in its path. Clasped together and paralyzed with fear, they stood frozen stiff as they became aware that the bird had trapped them in the hollow. There was a clearing directly in front of them with the enclave half mooned around them. There was no way out.

The bird headed directly for them. Alex's mind worked ferociously. She stepped back between the roots and found her body fall back against a stone wall. Straight away the wall swiveled around and deposited all of them safely on the other side. Plunged in total darkness they remained pinned against the wall. They might have escaped the bird but the situation presented a new challenge.

Alex frantically tried to untangle herself from a string of cobwebs that had her in a panic.

"Mum, Dad, Sam?" Her voice echoed back.

"Yeah, I'm here," Charles answered in a nervous voice, followed by a "Yip, I'm here too," from Sam and Izzy's faint ,"Me too."

"Okay great. Any chance any of you might have a flashlight or something?"

"I never leave home without one sweetheart," Charles chuckled retrieving a matchbox sized emergency flashlight from his pocket.

Seconds later the light from his torch shone across a dark chamber. The curtain of tree roots they had fallen through had disappeared, replaced by solid walls that encircled them. There were no doors or windows. The walls and floor were solid stone, and ancient engravings and abstract symbols lay splashed across them. Alex noticed an archaic flame torch against the wall and held it out to Sam.

"You have a match somewhere?"

"Matches and bandages Miss Hunt." He flicked the match against the stone wall and lit the flame.

Finally in a position to see their surroundings Alex ran toward her mother where Charles was already by her side.

"I can't believe you're alive! All this time we thought you were dead and he had you locked up in the safe house! I don't know why we never thought to go there. I'm truly sorry Mum."

"Hush sweet girl. You couldn't have known. The authorities were in on it."

"My dear Izzy, I should have known. What an idiot I've been?"

"We can't change it now, Charles. Let's not dwell on the past okay?"

She pulled away and looked across at Sam.

"Now, is someone going to introduce me to the young man who somehow landed himself in the middle of this?"

"Say me too. I hear he's a doctor," Charles joked.

"Yes, well he's a lot of things actually. This is Sam, Dr. Sam Quinn. He's Professor Keating's best student and also happens to be a qualified medical practitioner, yes. Oh, and quite possibly your biggest fan."

Sam blushed, visible even in the faint torchlight.

"I'm honored to meet you both Professor Hunt, Mrs. Hunt."

"A Doctor, that's quite something. Well, Dr. Quinn. It's a pleasure to meet you too."

"Oh, I forgot to mention, Sam is an aspiring archaeologist, so this is officially his first expedition."

"Thanks for the reminder, Alex. Now, if you don't mind me asking, where the heck are we and what was that thing that just chased us?"

Their laughter filled the hollow chamber.

"I haven't the foggiest Dr. Quinn. That thing was from the pits of hell if you ask me."

"Do you think it's the rapturous bird everyone's been talking about?" Sam asked Charles again.

"I don't know what else to think Sam. I've never seen anything like it. But if the rumors are true, then yes. It's quite possible. Perhaps a few simpler questions are where we are and how we are going to get out of here?"

"Well, it looks like some underground passageway. I have no idea how we got inside or how to get out. I can't see any doors," Alex cut in.

She ran her hand along the stone wall that had deposited them inside the chamber. There were no latches or openings.

"There's nothing here. I can't see any exit. Let's move this way."

Torch in hand, she moved forward ahead of them.

"Be careful Alexandra. There could be booby traps. These tunnels usually have snares everywhere."

Izzy barely finished her sentence before the floor gave away in front of Alex. Alex jumped sideways to avoid a sheer drop into a pit of darkness.

"That was close. Is everyone okay?" She didn't wait for anyone to answer. "We're going to have to try to balance along the wall on the ledge and then jump the last stretch. Do you think you can do this?" Alex nudged.

"Heck yeah, piece of cake," Sam said sarcastically.

"Like the doctor says. Piece of cake so let's go for it," Charles added.

The ledge was narrow and holding a firm footing wasn't easy, but they made it across. Alex lost her flame torch when the floor had given out and never heard it fall, declaring quite obviously the chasm's depth. As soon as she reached the other end, Charles tossed his torch across and started off on the ledge. In expert sequence they all moved safely along the ledge to the other end. When Sam, who was last, finally stepped off the ledge on the other side, it was as if someone had pushed a remote button and the stone floor straightaway closed up again behind them.

"I thought Egypt was tricky. That was a brush with death if ever I've seen one," Charles commented.

"Remarkable, it must operate on a weight switch," Izzy added.

"It feels good to have you with us, Izzy my love," Charles whispered to his wife.

"We're onto something here Dad. The raptor bird didn't want us coming in here. It was protecting it. All those dead people in its lair obviously came too close, burying the secret with them."

"You're right. Have a look at this, what do you make of it?"

Alex stared at a stone carving. It read:

Feed me, and I live, yet give me a drink, and I die

"I have no clue," Charles offered. "Everything lives with food but what will die with a drink? What drink? Alcohol? Poison?"

"Can you perhaps spot anything else anywhere that might help us decipher the riddle?" Izzy asked intrigued.

With the torch above their heads they held it up against the wall and inspected it block by block.

"Nope, only another torch that's bigger than this little one. Here, hold this please, Mum?" To Alex it was as if time had turned back and the famous Hunt team was as it was before her mother's deceitful death.

The larger torch cast an expansive glow across the entire passage.

"Mum, look!"

Painted on the wall was the raptor bird protecting a city adorned with gold and gems. Sketches of bags filled with spices and weapons lay scattered around an image of a temple.

"It's Rhapta, Mum! This is it! We found Rhapta!"

In that moment Alex couldn't ask for anything better. It had been a while since she felt that happy. The two people who meant most to her were right there with her. Not to mention that she had found a new best friend in Sam.

"There is a good chance here. It does look like it Alexandra, but I'm going to play it cool though okay? Let's not get ahead of ourselves. I'm still stuck on this riddle and let's not forget we need to find a way out of here."

Alex looked at the clue again.

"What dies when you give it a drink? Think. What liquid can kill?"

They paced back and forth until Sam eventually spoke.

"Well, water can kill a flame."

"Of course! Sam, you've actually got a nose for this. It's a fire." Charles patted a congratulatory hand on Sam's back, impressed with his quick thinking.

Sam sported a grin so wide that they expected his cheeks to crack any second. Alex burst with pride too. It was quite impressive that he had managed to crack the riddle. This man had undoubtedly changed her opinion from that first meeting on the plane.

"Okay, it's a fire. Now what? Are we supposed to light the torch above the riddle? That would be the 'burning a flame' part. What are we missing here?" Izzy queried.

Alex took a couple of steps back to have a better look at the wall around the riddle. A tiny furrow seemed to outline the puzzle and led all the way around the paintings on the wall. In the dark Alex wasn't able to see it clearly and moved the torch closer to the wall. Instantly the furrow caught alight and pushed the flame through the burrows along the walls. Like a massive labyrinth of golden passages made from fire it ran a trail throughout the chamber.

Charles expelled a loud gasp.

"Let's follow it. Look, it's carrying on over there," Alex yelled excitedly.

Before long they had followed the route through the tunnels where it stopped at tiny kindles of fire. In the center of the kindles, was a round pond filled with a thick liquid. Within seconds the pool exploded into a mass of flames and in turn ignited several other canals with fire. It was ancient ingenuity to the fullest. They were standing in a massive chamber, entirely illuminated by trenches of fire all around them.

"Mum, look there!"

They turned to where the fire had stopped and encircled an enormous shrine with a ring of fire. Above it was a gold statue of the soaring raptor bird they had run from earlier and in its claws, a rectangular box almost identical to the one they had found the scroll in. On this box, written in ancient Greek, it read

R-H-A-P-T-A

Izzy's legs collapsed from underneath her, as she fell to her knees and wept. Tears overwhelmed her when decades of searching finally came to pass.

"Is this true? After all these years of digging and believing in something we have not had any evidence of it existing and we finally found it!"

They had found Rhapta, yes. The ancient lost city of Africa was finally discovered.

"Yes Mum, you did it You REALLY did it. Your dream has come true and look, you're sitting right in front of it! You found Rhapta!"

Charles leapt to his wife's side. Sam, who stood mesmerized, eventually joined them in a celebratory huddle. The entire chasm was illuminated all around them, a shiny, glittering chamber.

"What do you think is in the box? Do you think it holds the treasures?" Alex eventually asked.

"I am convinced it looks precisely like the one we found. If it is, it can only mean that there's something hidden inside it. What it is, we are about to find out," Izzy ventured.

They stood in awe at the foot of the shrine, beneath the towering golden bird's claws.

"What if the thing comes to life when we touch the box? It could be booby-trapped, you know?" Alex paused.

"Not likely, my girl. I can't see anything indicating that it's alive. What I see though, is a box looking for a key."

"A key? Like a real key?" Sam piped up.

Izzy inspected it closer. "Certainly looks like it. The box resembles our one but look here. It's a hollow engraving of some sort. Almost as if we're supposed to place something on top of it to unlock it. I just don't know what yet. It's not very clear."

The box was perfection. Alex traced her fingers along the odd shape on top of the box. It looked familiar, very familiar. Her hand reached for the relic knife she hid in the small of her back before Sam and she left for the safe house.

"Well, knock me over with a feather! If it isn't the knife. The knife is the key! Alexandra, my clever girl. I think this time it's clear. You have your mother's brains after all."

Alex giggled. "Mum, you should do it."

Izzy took the knife from her daughter and placed it into the hollowed out shape on the side of the box. A series of loud clicking sounds filled the chamber all around them as they watched the box release latch after latch. And there, in front of their eyes, the box unlocked a drawer filled with gold coins and jewels of all descriptions.

And behind the shrine, a stone wall glided open to welcome the last of the day's bright rays to shine down on them.

CHAPTER EIGHTEEN

AFTER RHAPTA

The expansive auditorium gathered hundreds of archaeologists and scientists from around the world. Since discovering Rhapta, the smiles never left Charles Hunt's lips. His grin was now a permanent fixture of pride. Izzy never left his side either. She was never quite the same since their return and her three-year captivity haunted her each night, robbing her from her zest for life. Dr. Jones worked closely with her, but despite his efforts in getting her to open up, she plainly refused to talk about what had happened. And that was ok. She was alive.

Sam Quinn's calm presence was assuring to Alex as always. His never-ending strength and encouragement never ceased to amaze her and for the first time in a very long while, Alex Hunt found herself happy.

The auditorium fell silent before Professor Keating's voice echoed through the hall.

"And now, the moment we've all been waiting for. Please put your hands together for the courageous Alex Hunt!"

When the audience clapped and cheered as Alex took her place behind the podium, her tummy fluttered. She had hope. Hope in mankind, and hope in her future. She watched as Charles Hunt jumped to his feet with excitement, his wife safely by his side.

Sam Quinn's firm hand was in the small of her back next to her as he proudly stood behind her on the stage.

"You did great Alex Hunt," he whispered behind her ear.

They were a team now and she wouldn't want it any other way.

The crowd cheered and applauded with thunderous ovation as Alex invited Charles and Izzy to the stage with her. The Hunt Team did it again.

And when the crowd finally settled down, Professor Keating spoke a few words in honor of Charles.

"This is a bitter-sweet moment for us today. After years of loyal service to the university and the archaeology faculty, Professor Charles Hunt and his lovely wife, Izzy, will be entering retirement. They have endured and sacrificed much in their fight to preserve history and science and they will be sorely missed. We are fortunate enough that they've left us a legacy. One that will stand in their place and continue to carry the Hunt torch. Ladies and gentlemen, please welcome their courageous daughter, Alex Hunt!"

The crowd cheered as Alex stepped up to the microphone to deliver her speech. She cleared her throat in an attempt to hide her nerves.

"I stand before you today, a different woman, different in so many ways. Proud, grateful but above all, humbled. Because, not only have I found my Mum again, I am privileged to share this stage with *both* my parents and my best friend. You see, finding Rhapta wasn't just another quest after lost treasure. It was my Mum, Izzy Hunt's lifelong dream. She made it her life's goal and never gave up. Her determination and strength surpassed all, without which, none of this would have been possible. I'm different today because I've learned to never give up on your dreams. To push past your challenges and allow your passion to guide you. I'm different today because I've also learned not to rely on myself but to let people in. Vulnerability is good. Now, without further ado, ladies and gentlemen, The Hunt Team, is proud to share with you, our esteemed colleagues, the lost city of Rhapta!"

The audience was up on their feet again, this time silenced in awe. Behind the stage, the enormous, polished raptor sign lowered from the rafters. On either side of the stage, the projector screens displayed the multitude of photographs taken throughout the exploration and they watched mesmerized as the images told the story of their discovery. And when the crowd eventually dispersed to move between the displayed relics, Sam spoke quietly next to her side.

"You are one special woman, Alex Hunt. You had this bunch hanging onto your every word."

"Well, Sam Quinn. I couldn't have done it without you."

"So does this mean I can join you for the next hunt?"

"I think it's safe to say you are officially hired, Quinn. It wouldn't be much of an adventure without you."

He flashed a smile and planted a gentle kiss across the light pink scar on her forehead.

"My bags are packed, Alex Hunt. I'm ready to go wherever you wish to take me."

The ALEX HUNT Adventures continue in The GILDED TREASON. Available in eBook and Paperback **(https://books2read.com/ GILDED-TREASON)**

An ancient religious artifact. An international conspiracy. A mission that will put them through the ultimate test.

Some two thousand years ago, Buddha's remains were gathered in several golden urns and shared amongst his followers across the world. But, when one urn goes missing from a mountain shrine in Phnom Penh, the Cambodian government enlist the aid of formidable artifact salvagers Alex Hunt and Sam Quinn to hunt it down and return it to its holy place in the temple shrine.

Finding the golden urn was supposed to be easy; nothing the skilled pair hadn't done before. But little did Alex and Sam know they would become the center of an international conspiracy, a conspiracy so entangled in a web of secrets and crime that it could cost them their lives.

Faced with danger and underground syndicates, they soon realized they couldn't trust anyone. Nothing was as it seemed.

Join them in another riveting armchair adventure as they travel between Cambodia and Vietnam in an action-packed quest to uncover the truth!

Inspired by real historical facts and events. The Gilded Treason is Book 2 in the action-packed Alex Hunt Adventure Thriller series.

Also suitable as a standalone novel.

Receive a FREE copy of the prequel and see where it all started!

NOT AVAILABLE ANYWHERE ELSE!

Click on image or enter http://download.urcelia.com in your browser

MORE BOOKS BY URCELIA TEIXEIRA

ALEX HUNT Adventure Thrillers

Also suited as standalone novels

The PAPUA INCIDENT - Prequel (sign up to get it FREE)

The RHAPTA KEY

The GILDED TREASON

The ALPHA STRAIN

The DAUPHIN DECEPTION

The BARI BONES

The CAIAPHAS CODE

FREE BONUS - FOR YOUR EYES ONLY!

She's a highly skilled antiquities recoverer with the unrivaled ability to eradicate criminals in the archaeology world.

Receive an exclusive free copy of her classified files.

Available for your eyes only! (http://bit.ly/Meet-Alex-Hunt)

(Not available anywhere else!)

If you enjoyed this book, I would sincerely appreciate it if you could take the time to **leave a review**. It would mean so much to me!

For sneak previews, free books and more,

Join my mailing list

No-Spam Newsletter
ELITE SQUAD
(http://bit.ly/EliteSquadsignup)

FOLLOW Urcelia Teixeira

BookBub has a New Release Alert. Not only can you check out the latest deals, but you can also get an email when I release my next book by following me here

https://www.bookbub.com/authors/urcelia-teixeira

Website:
https://www.urcelia.com

Facebook:
https://www.facebook.com/urceliabooks

Twitter:
https//www.twitter.com/UrceliaTeixeira

ABOUT THE AUTHOR

Urcelia Teixeira is an author of fast-paced archaeological action-adventure novels with a Christian nuance.

Her Alex Hunt Adventure Thriller Series has been described by readers as 'Indiana Jones meets Lara Croft with a twist of Bourne'. She read her first book when she was four and wrote her first poem when she was seven. And though she lived vicariously through books, and her far too few travels, life happened. She married the man of her dreams and birthed three boys (and added two dogs, a cat, three chickens, and some goldfish!) So, life became all about settling down and providing a means to an end. She climbed the corporate ladder, exercised her entrepreneurial flair and made her mark in real estate.

Traveling and exploring the world made space for child-friendly annual family holidays by the sea. The ones where she succumbed to building sandcastles and barely got past reading the first five pages of a book. And on the odd occasion she managed to read fast enough to page eight, she was confronted with a moral dilemma as the umpteenth expletive forced its way off just about every page!

But by divine intervention, upon her return from yet another male-dominated camping trip, when fifty knocked hard and fast on her door, and she could no longer stomach the profanities in her reading material, she drew a line in the sand and bravely set off to create a new adventure!

It was in the dark, quiet whispers of the night, well past midnight late in the year 2017, that Alex Hunt was born.

Her philosophy

From her pen flow action-packed adventures for the armchair traveler who enjoys a thrilling escape. Devoid of the usual profanity and obscenities, she incorporates real-life historical relics and mysteries from exciting places all over the world. She aims to kidnap her reader from the mundane and plunge them into feel-good riddle-solving quests filled with danger, sabotage, and mystery!

For more visit www.urcelia.com or email her on books@urcelia.com

facebook.com/urceliateixeira

twitter.com/urcelia_teixeira

instagram.com/urceliateixeira

CONTENTS

Special Thanks	iii
Preface	vii
Chapter 1	1
Chapter 2	21
Chapter 3	39
Chapter 4	55
Chapter 5	73
Chapter 6	89
Chapter 7	107
Chapter 8	125
Chapter 9	141
Chapter 10	157
Chapter 11	173
Chapter 12	191
Chapter 13	203
Chapter 14	219
Chapter 15	229
Chapter 16	239
Chapter 17	255
Chapter 18	273
More books by Urcelia Teixeira	281
FREE BONUS - FOR YOUR EYES ONLY!	283
About the Author	287
Disclaimer & Copyright	291

DISCLAIMER & COPYRIGHT

DISCLAIMER & COPYRIGHT

Paperback © ISBN: 978-0-6399665-0-2

Independently Published by Urcelia Teixeira

www.urcelia.com

books@urcelia.com

Made in the USA
Columbia, SC
23 October 2021